Kingpin Killaz

Lock Down Publications and Ca$h
Presents
Kingpin Killaz
A Novel by *Hood Rich*

Kingpin Killaz

Lock Down Publications
P.O. Box 870494
Mesquite, Tx 75187

Visit our website @
www.lockdownpublications.com

Copyright 2018 KINGPIN KILLAZ

First Edition November 2018
Printed in the United States of America

Lock Down Publications
Like our page on Facebook: Lock Down Publications @
www.facebook.com/lockdownpublications.ldp
Cover design and layout by: **Dynasty Cover Me**
Book interior design by: **Shawn Walker**
Edited by: **Lauren Burton**

Stay Connected with Us!

Text **LOCKDOWN** to 22828 to stay up-to-date with new releases, sneak peaks, contests and more…

Thank you.

Submission Guideline.

Submit the first three chapters of your completed manuscript to ldpsubmissions@gmail.com, subject line: Your book's title. The manuscript must be in a .doc file and sent as an attachment. Document should be in Times New Roman, double spaced and in size 12 font. Also, provide your synopsis and full contact information. If sending multiple submissions, they must each be in a separate email.

Have a story but no way to send it electronically? You can still submit to LDP/Ca$h Presents. Send in the first three chapters, written or typed, of your completed manuscript to:

LDP: Submissions Dept
Po Box 870494
Mesquite, Tx 75187

DO NOT send original manuscript. Must be a duplicate.

Provide your synopsis and a cover letter containing your full contact information.

Thanks for considering LDP and Ca$h Presents.

Hood Rich

6

Chapter 1

My eyelids felt heavier than cinder blocks as I struggled to keep them open. The windshield wipers swished back and forth on my father's 2019 Mercedes Benz truck. Air from the vents blew directly into my face until I adjusted them. My stomach growled for the fifth time as my father handed me a stuffed Garcia Vega filled with Chicago Kush. I took it and inhaled a deep breath before putting it to my lips and taking a strong pull. The reflection of the cherry on the blunt appeared in the side window along with my puffed out jaws.

My father, Castro, looked over at me with low eyelids and smiled. "That's that heat right there, ain't it, son? Look at you, you can barely keep your eyes open." He laughed and nodded his head.

My father was a caramel-skinned man. He had brown eyes with a slightly rounded face. For as long as I could remember, he'd always kept his facial hair cut into a goatee. It was slightly graying. He had a bald head that he kept that way because his hair was light on top, so he wore fitted caps with NBA team logos on them. My father was 5'11" tall and weighed about two hundred pounds solid.

I coughed up a cloud of smoke and beat on my chest. It felt like my lungs were on fire. I shook my head and handed him back the blunt. "Pop, I'm high as hell. I don't know where you got this kill from. Yesterday, I traveled all the way down to Englewood just to get some halfway mediocre bag, but it ain't got nothing on this. Straight up." I grabbed my juice from the console and took a long swallow. "So, what's the game plan?"

The rain continued to pelt down on the top of the truck's hood. It sounded like rocks were dropping on top of it. It was raining so hard I could barely see out the windshield. It looked like we were going through a car wash. Thunder growled in the sky before an electric bolt shot across it. It illuminated the dark streets. It was one in the morning on what had been a hot and sticky day.

My father turned down the Isley Brothers track bellowing out of the speakers. "Like I told you before, son, I handled everything with them boys on the west side. We're good to go long as everybody holds up their ends. We should be able to move out to Jackson Drive and set up shop in the row houses out that way. I got ten bricks in the trunk, and there is another five back home in Riverdale. The reason I brought you out here tonight is because I need you to watch my back after I make this deal. It's for a hundred and fifty thousand, altogether. You know yo' old man can't be rolling around Chicago with that type of dough and not expect trouble." He took a pull from the blunt before crushing it out in the ashtray.

"Well, I'm out here wit' you, Pops. I don't care what go on, you got my word I ain't about to let nothing happen to you."

"I know you won't, son. That's why I called you to have my back. I still can't believe how much you've turned into what I used to be, though. Every time I look at yo' ass I can't do nothin' but shake my head." He stopped at the light on Halstead. "Two hundred more thousand and I'll finally be able to buy the church for your mother. I been promising her this for the last ten years, son. It's time I live up to my promises and make them happen for her. I'm ready to turn over a new leaf myself. I can't be in these streets forever." He pulled off at the green light and turned left, heading down the avenue.

"I still can't understand how y'all have even managed to gel this long. Mama is a pastor of a church, and you've been a dope boy ever since you two were in high school. How does that even work?" I was so high I was started to nod a little bit. Not only did I have the Chicago Kush in my system, but I was goin' off two Mollies and a half bottle of Lean. I was fucked up and struggling to stay lucid. I needed to keep my old man talking or I was going to fall asleep on his ass.

"Your mother didn't find out I was hustling until only a few years ago. Even then she didn't know the logistics, and she still doesn't. Our relationship has worked thus far because I have always respected your mother. I've always allowed her to chase her dreams and tried my best to support her. We live by a system where we don't ask questions unless we are sure we're able to live with the consequences or reality each of us has outside of one another. I think a part of her has always known about my lifestyle, but she's never really wanted to know the truth because then she'd be forced to make a decision between me and her faith. She always said a believing wife can sanctify her husband as long as she is in alignment with God. Your mother always has been."

My head fell forward as my eyelids closed slowly. I didn't jerk my neck backward until I saw the dashboard about to connect with my face. I sat back in the seat and turned the air conditioner vent so it blew on my face again. "That's what's up, Pops. I applaud you and Mom's union. I always have."

He laughed. "Then why you ain't thought about getting yourself right so you can marry Yaniece? She's a good girl, son, and she loves you to death. I can see she ain't gon' take no shit from you, but that's a good thing. You need a strong woman to stand beside you so she can uplift you when you're feeling weak. And call you on your bullshit when you're feeling to big for your britches. I see a lot of your mother in Yani."

I waved him. "Nall, she just my homie right now. I'm only twenty-five. I ain't ready for all that relationship stuff just yet. I'm trying to keep my barbershops running the right way and make sure I can cop the Fifty Yard Line nightclub when Devon move out to Baltimore next year. I'ma turn that joker into a boss strip club with nothing but the finest dimes in all of Chicago. Once I get it to popping, I'm looking to expand. I got dreams, Pops. I ain't trying to be in the streets forever."

He looked over at me and smiled. "You got your

business degrees, son. Put them to use. One thing about the game is you always have to have an exit strategy. This shit don't last forever. My end game is to finally become a Kingdom man beside your mother in the church. It's my time, son. I feel the game weighing heavy on my spirit."

He made a right and pulled into the Altgeld Gardens Row Housing Projects, grabbed his .40 Glock from under his seat, and placed it into the holster under his left arm. "I hope these niggas ain't all doped up and shit here. I'm trying to be in and out."

I ran my hand over my face and sat up straight in my seat. "Aw, you out here messing wit' these niggas in the Garden? Damn, Pops, you should have told me that." I took off my seatbelt as he pulled into a parking spot in front of the row houses. The rain seemed to pick up its strength. The ground looked like a shallow swimming pool as more and more droplets fell onto it. I could smell the scent of rain in the air.

He took off his seatbelt and grabbed the book bag from the back seat. "Don't trip. I know it's a lot of stuff that been going on out here, but me and these dudes got an understanding. They're at war, but as long as we're in and out, we shouldn't be affected by it."

It was raining so hard I couldn't even make out the buildings in front of us. Suddenly, there was a banging on the top of the car, catching me off guard. Then the car was surrounded by a bunch of dudes in bomber jackets with hoods pulled over their heads. One in particular knocked on my father's window with the butt of his gun. I slid my hand into my coat and clutched my .45. I was ready to start busting if it came down to that.

Altgeld Gardens was notorious for stick-up kids, and murders. Why my father had chosen to do business with these niggas was beyond me.

He turned the interior lights on and held his hands at shoulder-height. "Heinous, just chill, son. I know your trigger finger is itching, but this is standard procedure for these dudes out here. They ain't doing nothing we should take personal." He rolled down the window just enough for the man to stick his face inside of it.

"What up, Jo? Fuck you niggas doing in our parking lot?" the man asked with half of his face covered by a blue rag.

"We come to do business with Freeman. I'm Castro. He should be expecting me."

The masked dude leaned his head further into the window. "Nigga, I've been put up on your pending arrival, but who the fuck is that over there?" He pointed in my direction.

"That's my son, and I brought him along because he's my business partner. Once again, Freeman already hip to all of this, young blood. All you gotta do is let him know we're here."

The man jerked his head back as if he was offended. Lightning flashed through the sky behind him. Rain popped off of his shoulder and into the car.

"Nigga, you got me fucked up. I know you ain't sitting yo' old ass in this car making it seem like you're frustrated with me or giving me orders. If that's the case, I'll morgue you right here. You and that nigga over there. Freeman don't run this bitch no more. I do. I'm his son, and the Gardens belong to me. Either respect that or lose yourself to the morgue. Which is it gon' be?"

I got heated right away. I didn't give a fuck how many niggas he had surrounding our car, I wasn't about to let nobody talk to my old man like that in my presence. "Say, homie, you can ice all that tough shit wit' my pops, nigga. Like he said, we come over here to handle some bidness wit' yo' father. Muthafuckas ain't looking for no trouble, but I ain't ducking no action, either. It's Englewood in this bitch." I sat up straight in my seat, ready to blow at this nigga if I had to.

"Fuck-boy, I don't give a fuck who he is to you or what you want out of me. Fuck him, and fuck you. This ain't no muthafucking Englewood out here, homie. This the wild, wild hunnits. Land of murder. Y'all are about to become the next victims in this bitch."

"Pops, pull off. Fuck this nigga. They on bullshit."

My father shook his head. "Nall, son, this deal has to go down tonight. I need to meet with the bank early tomorrow afternoon. I gotta give your mother this cash so she can convert it. It ain't no time for all of this bickering back and forth." He held up a hand to me and turned to face Freeman's son. "Say, I apologize for my son and for how we just rolled up in here. That's my bad. If you can look past that transgression, then we'd like to continue along with our business arrangement we have with your father. I'm sure what I'll be giving him is only going to make y'all's hood more productive."

He took a step back and allowed the rain to beat down on his hood. He leaned to his right and whispered something into the ear of one of the members of his crew. The other man nodded and disappeared from the scene, then Freeman's son stepped back up to my father's window and leaned down. "I just sent word to my old man to see what the move is. Long as he say you niggas are good, then y'all can proceed forward. But next time y'all come through this bitch, you ask for Pesos first. That's me. Once I give my permission, and only when, will you be able to conduct any business in the Gardens. You niggas got that?" he asked, looking at my father, then over to me.

My Pops nodded his head. "We got it, li'l homie. That mistake won't happen again. You got my word on that."

"What about you, fuck-boy? You heard what the fuck I just said?" he asked, leaning so far into the window the rain from his hood dropped onto my father's lap.

"I don't fuck wit' you niggas out here, so it won't be a next time. Far as all that slick shit you spitting, I ain't feeling nor honoring none of it. You need to take some communication courses or something. You trying to cost your old man a lot of money." I picked up my juice and took a nice swallow from it once again.

Pesos grunted and nodded his head. "Yeah, I see you one of them real Tough Tony-ass niggas, huh? Yeah, a'ight, it's a grave yard full of niggas like you. I keep that muthafucka in bidness. You catching my drift, Jo?"

I laughed to myself and clenched my jaw over and over again. I was getting vexed, ready to snap the fuck out. My high was wearing off, and I was getting a headache. Those were two reasons alone for me to be in a fucked-up mood. "Yeah, nigga, you ain't the only one wit' a body count."

"Hey, why don't y'all chill, Heinous? Damn. Let's just handle this business and get out of here. It's that simple," my father snapped with a mug on his face.

Pesos, laughed. "Listen to your old man, nigga. You might be able to roll up out this bitch wit' ya life." He sucked his teeth.

The man whose ear he'd whispered into came back and tapped him on the shoulder. He stood up and they stepped away from the truck, whispering as the rain fell onto them.

"Pop, I'm telling you, we should get up out of here. These niggas is on bullshit. How are you not seeing this?" I asked, feeling appalled. How could my old man have been in the game for so long and not smell danger when it was right in his face?

"No, they're not, son. It's just how they do business. I gotta get your mother that church. She deserves it," he said slightly under his breath.

I was so angry by this point I didn't even respond. I turned up the Isley Brothers track and sat back in my seat.

Pesos stuck his head back in the window. "Yeah, my old man said you should give me the work. I'll take it to him and bring you back the money. So, let's do that."

My father frowned. "What? Nigga, you gotta be out of yo' fucking mind. What I look like?" he asked, placing his hand on the gear shift.

Pesos took a step back, and the next thing I knew there was a shotgun pointed to my father's temple. Pesos pumped it. "You look like a dead body if you don't step yo' bitch-ass out of the truck, old man. Welcome to the Gardens, baby."

My heart felt like it leapt out of my chest. I could barely breathe. My palms were itchy and sweaty at the same time. My throat felt like it was sore. "I told you," I shouted.

"Get yo' bitch ass out of the truck, old man! Hurry the fuck up!" The members of his crew started to beat on the hood of the truck. There was a steady tapping on my passenger's side window from the handle of a gun.

My father shook his head. "Nall, son. I can't let us go out like this. That nigga Freeman must've set me up."

"Get yo' ass out of the truck, old man. I ain't

16

gon' tell you again!" Pesos hollered. He took the shotgun and busted into the air. *Boom*. The bright light from the fire out of his barrel illuminated the parking lot.

As soon as the shot went off, my window shattered. Glass splashed all over my face and chest. I pulled the .45 from my waist and turned in the direction of my window when a bullet shot into my shoulder, and then one went into my back, throwing me against my father. It felt like I was being stung by the biggest bee in the world. The stinging kept on getting worse and worse as I felt my blood pouring out of me.

Hood Rich

Chapter 2

My father threw the truck into reverse and slammed on the gas.

Boom.

Peso squeezed the trigger on the shotgun, blowing off half of my old man's face. It splashed against the windshield like strawberry snow cone ice. His body landed in my lap. He shook like a fish out of water while his blood saturated me. The truck sped backward at full speed until it crashed into a big, green dumpster. The back window shattered from the impact.

Bocka. Bocka. Bocka. Boom. Boom. Boom. Boom came the bullets from Pesos and his crew. The truck rocked back and forth under the attack. I could hear my father choking on his own blood. My lap felt like I'd peed on myself, but I'd done no such thing. I knew without a shadow of a doubt it was the blood of my father.

Boom. Boom. Boom. Bocka. Bocka. Bocka. Bocka. More shots rang in our direction. My back felt numb. My shoulder felt like it was slowly being ripped off. The pain was unbearable. I could hear their footsteps splashing in the water of the parking lot. I had to get my father off me before they made it over to us. I could smell that he'd released his bowels. The scent of feces was heavy in the air, along with copper.

I grabbed my gun and placed it in my left hand, pulled my father to the floor of the truck, and climbed over him as best I could. As soon as I made it to the driver's seat, the whole front windshield shattered. Rain poured in on me, drenching me almost immediately.

Shots rang in my direction, one flying past my ear and shattering the back window. I felt like I was about to die from a bullet or a panic attack. The heat was on, and thanks to my father, I had not been prepared for it. I raised the .45 and fired in their direction, at the same time throwing the truck in drive and slamming on the gas, feeling the wheels spinning up under me.

Boom. Boom. Boom. Boom. I busted and turned the wheel to the right on my way out of the parking lot.

Bocka. Bocka. Bocka. Boom. Boom. Boom.

Ssssss! The back tire of the truck deflated, causing the truck to tilt to one side. I didn't give a fuck. I had to get out of there.

Bullets ricocheted off of the truck as I hopped a curb and found myself in the middle of the street on 131st and South Evans. Once in the street, I floored the gas and sped away with blood leaking out of me. I felt dizzy and giddy at the same time. More shots rang out in my direction. Rain poured in on me from outside.

As I got to the corner, two men ran out to block my path with assault rifles in their hands. My eyes got as big as saucers before the shots spat rapidly, putting big holes in the truck's exterior. I ducked as low as I could and kept my foot on the gas.

I sped out into the busy intersection and made a right on my way to my mother's home.

***

I don't know how I managed to make it there, but as soon as I pulled up to my mother's home, I fainted and fell on the horn of the truck. It blared loudly in the night. I could no longer keep my eyes open.

I woke up three hours later and found I was inside the emergency room at the hospital. I'd been turned onto my side, and there was a big white patch on my shoulder. I could feel my back was taped up as well. I was high as a kite, but I could still feel the pain from the bullets.

I looked to my left to find Yaniece sitting in the chair alongside my bed with a Kleenex in one hand and her phone in the other. She saw my eyes were open and jumped out of her seat, rushing to my side.

"Baby, baby, baby. Oh my God, your father is dead. He's dead, baby. They killed him. I thought they'd killed you, too," she cried, grabbing my hand and kissing it.

At hearing that revelation, I became sick. I felt like I'd been punched in the gut by reality. Though my emotions were clogged, I couldn't help but feel angry. "Where is he at, Yani?"

"Where is who at, baby? Are you talking about your father? I just told you, he's gone, bae." She turned her head to the side as if she was confused.

I moved my right arm just a little bit and wanted to holler out in agony. I winced and bit into my lower lip. "I know he's gone. Don't say that shit no more. I get that. I'm asking you where do they have him?" I tried to sit up so I could face her better. I didn't feel comfortable lying on my side, either.

She scrunched her face. "He's with the coroner. Damn. I been sitting hear worried sick about you, and then when you get on up, this is how you act? Damn, Heinous," she snapped.

I slowly turned and placed the left side of my back on the pillow. "Calm down, man. I just lost my fucking father. I ain't trying to be beefing wit' yo' ass right now. Just tell me what's going on. I feel like I can barely remember anything." I clenched my teeth and closed my eyes before opening them to look at her. My head was spinning like crazy.

"Your mother say she found you and your father in his truck. He was already dead, and you were lying on the steering wheel with blood pouring out of you. I was at home, asleep, when she called me and told me to meet her here. She didn't tell me what had taken place over the phone. All she kept on saying was 'there's been an accident,' and you and Castro were seriously hurt. Do you know what that does to a person? The suspense? The worry I've had for you until you just woke up, right now?" She balled her hands into fists and took a deep breath. "I'm tired of going through this shit. It's always something with you and this fucking city. I thought we were moving away from here soon. Or has that changed?"

22

Yani was 5'3" tall and a bi-racial mix of black and Mexican. She had light brown eyes and a mole on the left side of her upper lip, along with gorgeous, long, silky black hair and a body to die for. She was a money-getting stripper and all about her paper and independence. Her only soft spot was me, and vice versa. We'd been fucking around with each other ever since my senior year when I'd transferred from Fenger High School to Roosevelt out in the wild hundreds, where I currently stayed.

Even though she was my woman, we really didn't have any hooks into each other like that. She was free to roam, and so was I. I had feelings for her and all that good shit, but I didn't know where I wanted to take them just yet. Life, to me, was way too short, plus I loved pussy more than oxygen. The thicker the bitch, the better.

"A'ight, that's my fault, shorty. I'm just fucked up over my pops, that's all. Come over here and give me a kiss on my cheek. These bullets got me twisted right now. I need some healing."

She pursed her lips. "Uh-huh. I shouldn't give yo' evil-ass nothin'. Where is all them hos you got at right now? See, yo' mama ain't think to call them. She called me. That should tell yo' black ass something." She came over and kissed my lips, holding my chin with her thumb and forefinger.

The scent of her perfume floated up my nose. Her tongue tasted like toothpaste and Double Mint gum. Her lips were juicy. We smacked loudly as we got into it. I was able to escape for thirty seconds while the kiss lasted.

It was broken up by the sound of knocking on the door. Before I could answer, a dark-skinned man dressed in black pants and a white shirt stepped into the room with a badge on the right side of his pants. "Can I come in?" he asked, closing the door behind him. He stood about 6'4" tall, had a shiny bald head, and a bushy mustache.

"Hell nall, you can't come in my fucking room. Get yo' ass up out of here. I ain't got shit to say," I snapped. If it was one group of animals I didn't trust in this world, it was the Chicago Police Force. In my opinion, they were dirtier than any other force in the united states. I'd had more than a few of my homies murdered by them in cold blood, and another bunch were doing time for crimes they didn't commit. They'd been set up by the dirty cowards who were a part of the Chicago Law Enforcement.

I personally hated anything with a badge, even the security guards in stores.

The bald-headed cop smiled. "Oh, I'm sorry. I must've made it seem like you had a choice. Li'l girl, you need to step outside while I get some answers from this idiot who's lucky to be alive," he laughed. He pulled out a five-inch tablet and turned it on.

"Fuck you, I ain't going nowhere. I don't trust you dirty cowards to not do something to my man. He's vulnerable right now. I'm here to protect him until he can protect himself. That's just what it is." Yani stepped closer to me and interlocked her fingers within my own. She had a frown on her face and was turning red.

"Yeah, nigga. Anything you got to ask me, you can ask me in front of my jewel. I ain't got shit to hide." I looked him up and down.

A smirk came across his face. "Oh, you one of them types, huh? You gotta act all hard in front of your ghetto queen, huh? Yeah, I get it. Let me ask you a question: you think she gon' be able to save yo' ass if I take you down to the Cook County Jail and let all them rivals get all up in your back door? Yeah, you come in there all fucked up like this, by the time you leave you'll be sweeter than a packet of sugar," he laughed.

My face was balled into an angry snarl. "Fuck you, pork chop. G'on 'head and ask yo' questions. My baby ain't going nowhere."

He shrugged his shoulder. "A'right then, suit yourself. Can you tell me what happened tonight?"

I shook my head. "Nope. I don't remember. I guess with all the blood lost, it affected my memory."

"Can you tell me where you were when you and your father were shot? There looks to be more than a hundred holes in his truck but, ironically, we didn't receive any calls from the area about shots being fired. Not only that, but the shots-fired detectors didn't go off in your mother's neighborhood, which means you had to bring this drama to her home. So, where did you come from?"

"I don't know what the fuck you talking about. All I know is I woke up here. Anything that happened before that, I can't tell you about. You wasting your

25

time."

"Yeah, man, why don't you go fake like you working in somebody else room? Even if you knew who did this shit, you wouldn't do nothing about it. Ain't nobody got time for y'all games," Yani said with her eyes lowered into slits. She'd watched her brother only two summers ago be gunned down by the Chicago Police. They'd killed him in a case of mistaken identity. One of the officers had gone so far as to place a dirty gun on his person so the media would broadcast that fact and it would take away from the wrong they'd caused her family and the laws they'd violated.

Detective Taylor shook his head. "Y'all some dirty, dumb niggers. It's amazing just how dumb you muthafuckas truly are. You kill each other all day long, and then be ready to bite my head off when I try and do my job. Just ignorant. I hate you bitches."

"Aye, man, watch yo' mouth, nigga. I don't give a fuck about that punk-ass badge. You keep acting like you from the streets, I'ma treat you like you are, homeboy. Now, we don't need yo' help. Take yo' punk-ass to a doughnut shop or something. You're the enemy just as much as these people who shot him. You ain't fooling nobody. You're a wolf in sheep's clothing. All of you pigs are."

Detective Taylor scoffed and shook his head. "That's a damn shame. Y'all too stupid even know how dumb you really are. He gon' let somebody kill his father and nearly take his life, then refuse to cooperate with me so I can put the son of a bitch behind bars for the rest of his life. I just don't get it." He turned off his tablet and put it back into his pocket.

"It ain't for you to get, homie. You're on the other side. You're an adversary. You'd try and kill me just as fast as one of my enemies on the street. I ain't fucking wit' you, Jo, so keep it moving."

He nodded. "Oh, I will. You gotta bury your father and hope you recover from them slugs, not me. If you too stupid to seek help, then that's on you. Both of y'all can kiss my well-protected ass. I see you in the city morgue soon. I'm sure of that." He stepped out of the room and slammed the door behind him.

"Argh!" Yani hollered and balled her hands into fists. "I hate them muthafuckas. I swear to God, I do. Every time I see one of those pigs, it make me think about Greg. My brother was only thirteen years old, Heinous. He was a good kid. He ain't never hurt nobody, and they shot him down in the street like a fucking rabid dog. I can still remember it like it was yesterday. My mother ain't been right ever since." She stood in the middle of the floor, staring off into the distance.

My mother knocked on the door, then rushed into the room. She took my face into her hands. "My baby. Baby, are you okay?" she cried with tears dripping down her cheeks.

My mother was a caramel-skinned woman with a short hairstyle that accentuated her wavy hair texture. She had brown eyes and a slender face and body. She

27

was my heart and my first love in life, no matter what took place.

"I'm good, Ma. They tried to rob us, and if I hadn't gotten behind the wheel after they shot me and did this to my Pops, then I'd be lying in the morgue as well. I'm so sorry for your loss, Ma. I swear I am." I opened my arms for her to come in between them. I hugged her as tight as I could, fighting through the pain.

"They killed him, honey. Your father was about to leave the game, and they killed him. I can't believe something like this would happen to him. It isn't fair," she cried with her face in my chest.

I was never able to shed tears, even as a little kid, until I saw my mother crying. Then it was like the dam to my emotions couldn't help but be released. I felt the water coming down my cheeks and wiped it away. The reality that my father was gone was finally coming at me full-force. I felt sick.

"He was about to leave the game alone, son. Now he's gone. Why would God allow for this to happen at the end? I don't understand it, and I gotta take this to my prayer closet." She cried harder into my chest and balled my hospital gown into her fist.

Yani stepped behind her and rubbed her back. "I'm here for you, Mrs. Green. Anything you need me to do, please don't hesitate to ask me. I loved Castro like a father. He was a good man." She laid her head on my mother's back.

"Thank you, baby, but I don't even know how I'm going to make it out of tonight. I feel like I've lost the best part of me."

I lay there in the bed, holding my mother and feeling her shake against me. I felt like I could kill everybody that lived in the Gardens, innocent people and all. I'd never felt more like a victim in my whole life. Not only had I lost my father and been shot twice, but now my mother was losing herself and coming apart at the seams.

I had to make Pesos and Freeman pay. I had to fuck them over worse than they'd screwed over my family. I didn't care how powerful they were or how many soldiers were running under them. I wanted to crush them by any means.

At the same time, I had to find a way to buy my mother her church. I felt like my father had beaten it into my brain prior to his death. It felt like it was his dying request, and I had to step up to the plate and make it happen for him.

***

We buried my father seven days later. I refused to attend the funeral. I didn't want to be around a bunch of crying people making it seem like my father's death was the worst thing that could have possibly happened to them. I wasn't with that fake shit. It would only piss me off and increase the anger I felt deep within the pit of my soul.

So, instead, I waited until the cemetery cleared out before I walked over to my old man's grave and sat down beside it with a big blunt of Chicago Kush in my hand, already blazed. I untwisted the cap on my Hennessy and poured some on top of his casket, which was already lowered into the ground. The sun had already set, but the humidity was crazy. I had sweat along my forehead, and my bulletproof vest was sticking to me. I took a swallow of the Hennessy and wiped my mouth with the back of my hand, took a deep breath, and looked down into the grave.

"Damn, Pops. I knew them niggas had something up their sleeves. I felt it deep in my soul. I wished you would have listened, though. I think your biggest downfall was you were too trusting." I took a strong pull from the Kush and inhaled it deeply. "I'ma get them niggas, though. Ain't no muthafucking way I'ma let 'em get away with what they did to us, but especially you. I know I may have never told you this, even as a little kid, but you were something like my hero, old man. Ever since I was old enough to understand how you were moving and grooving out here in these streets, I been looking up to you."

I lowered my head and smacked a big mosquito that had landed on my forearm. It was already filled with blood, and I was hoping it wasn't mine. Mosquitoes were carrying all types of diseases these days. There was a full moon in the sky. Crickets chirped in the distance, and I could hear traffic along the highway only a few blocks over from the graveyard.

I stood up and placed my hand on his plot. "Pop, on everything I love, I'ma crush these niggas and become what you never could in these streets. I won't fail, and I ain't about to submit to no nigga. I'ma get Moms that Church, too. Probably even wife Yani after I get this lust bug out of my system. That's somewhere down the line, though, so chill with the rush on that." I laughed and teared up at the same time. My throat felt as if it had a lump of coal directly in the center of it. I had a hard time swallowing. "I just want to let you know I love you, Pops, and I appreciate you for being my father. It's a whole lot of niggas out here that ain't never had one, but thanks to you, I've never had to be one of them. My love for you is forever sealed in blood. I got our family. I'ma put Moms and Leah on my back and make it happen for this family. That's my word to you as a man and as a son. Hold ya head up there. I got this down here."

I jumped and dropped my drink and blunt when I felt a presence closing in on me. By the time I got my pistol off my hip, I saw the gravedigger standing about twenty feet away with his hands in the air.

"Say, Jo, I don't want no trouble. I was just coming to finish my job. That's it, li'l brother. I got a wife and three kids at home. Please don't take my life," the heavyset, dark-skinned man said with sweat dropping off of his chin.

I kept my gun aimed at him for longer than I should have. After being shot twice and losing my father, I was on constant edge. My heart pounded in my chest.

He slowly got down on both knees with his hands still in the air. "I'm begging you. Please."

I shook my head, yet kept my gun aimed at him.

"Get the fuck out of here. I ain't done talking to my old man yet. Can't you see this shit!=? Huh, muthafucka?" I cocked the hammer. "Go!"

He jumped to his feet and took off running, looking back over his shoulder every now and then, I assumed, to make sure I wasn't chasing him.

I lowered the gun and looked into my father's grave. The tears started to pour like a broken geyser.

Chapter 3

I didn't feel like I was strong enough to get back on my grind until three weeks later. I was still fucked up. My shoulder was killing me, and my right arm had this thing where it'd go numb out of the blue and stay that way for a full two to three minutes, and there was nothing I could do about it. For some reason I couldn't help the sick feeling in my stomach. Anytime I would try to put something hot in my stomach, minutes later I would wind up throwing it up. I grew miserable quickly. It got so bad during those three weeks that all I wanted to do was lie in the bed and smoke Kush.

Even though I'd told Yani I wanted to be alone because I was going through some shit, she showed up on the 22 day at 11 o'clock at night with a Prada book bag draped over her shoulders. When I answered the door, instead of her waiting for me to invite her in, she simply stepped right past me, talking a mile a minute.

"Look, I don't want to hear no bullshit from you, Heinous. I know what you told me, but I don't care. I'm here, and you're going to deal with it." She sat her book bag on the couch and unzipped her spring jacket, looking into my eyes the entire time. "Say what you gon' say so we can move on," she dared.

I closed the door after looking both ways into the night, locked it, and ran my hands over my waves. "Shorty, I ain't got the energy to be fighting with you. How have you been?" I stepped past her and into the living room where I had the Lakers game playing. I had to watch LeBron do his thing even though I was feeling some type of way about him being out west now.

She stepped up to me and stood in my face. "I can't get a kiss or nothing? Damn, you ain't been fucking wit' me on Facebook, either. You making me feel like I'm the enemy."

I shook my head. "It ain't nothing like that. I'm just trying to get my head right, that's all." I held her chin and planted a sensual kiss on her juicy lips. She moaned into my mouth and swiped her tongue across my lips.

"Look, Heinous, I know you going through it right now but, baby, I need some of my man. I'm horny as fuck, and I ain't trying to fuck wit' none of these nasty-ass Chicago niggas. I need some of you. It might be what you need, as well, to pull you out of that funk you're in." She reached between my legs and cupped my penis, squeezing it in her hand.

I turned her around so her big booty was in my lap. She had on a real short, pink skirt that stopped at the top of her thick thighs. Once turned around, I sucked on the side of her neck and ran my hand down her stomach. "So, I'm thinking you came over here to make sure I was good, but it turns out its all about you, huh?" I sucked on her neck and continued to raise her skirt until it was above her hips, then I slid my hand into her panties. I was met by bald, hot, puffy pussy lips that had moisture seeping out of them. I played with the juices on my fingers.

She pressed her ass further into my lap and spread her feet apart. "Daddy, can you let me ride that dick right quick? I just need to get right. My hole killing me." She ran her tongue over her lips and sucked on the bottom one.

I slid two fingers up her box and pulled them in and out of her. After the fifth insertion they were dripping wet, so much so that her essence trailed down my wrist. "You trying to get on Daddy, right? If I let you get up here, what you gon' do?" I teased, fingering her a little faster. She bucked forward into my fingers, shaking. "You. Already. Know. What. I'ma do. I'm a beast," she moaned, spreading her thighs further apart.

I slipped my fingers out of her and sucked her juices off of them. I slid them back into her for three strokes and pulled them back out. "Huh, taste yourself."

"No, I don't want to," she whined. "I want you to fuck me, Heinous. Damn."

I bit into her neck and scraped at it with my teeth before sucking it harder. I slipped my fingers back inside of her and pulled them back out. "Taste this pussy so Daddy can do his thing. Come on, ma. You know how this shit go." I placed my fingers on her juicy lips.

She groaned and then sucked them into her mouth, licking up and down them. "Mm, Daddy, you happy now?" she asked, licking into the cracks on my hand.

I threw her over the arm of the couch and yanked

her skirt upward. She yelped as her yellow ass cheeks jiggled into the open. I dropped down to my knees and ran my face all over her globes before sucking her pussy through the crotch band of her red, satin panties. They were drenched. Juices ran down her thighs all the way to her slender ankles. I licked upward and yanked her panties to the side. Her pussy looked like an open rose from the back. The lips were a golden brown, her insides a glossy bubblegum pink. I stuck my nose on her hole and inhaled.

"Go, Daddy. Go. Eat that thang back there. Please." She held her ass cheeks apart to give me better access.

I opened her lips and sucked on her erect clitoris, running my tongue in circles around it over and over. She jerked and spread her legs apart. Half of her body was bent over the couch. She pulled up her T-shirt to expose her double-D breasts, the nipples a cherry brown, fully elongated. I watched her pinch and pull on the right one while she tried her best to look back at me. "Uh! Daddy. Yes! Do that shit! Fuck, yes!"

My tongue darted in and out of her, stabbing and tasting her inner essence. Her juice ran down my chin and neck. I sucked at her lips, pulling them into my mouth loudly before sliding three fingers up her and running them in and out at full speed while my teeth nipped at her clitoris.

She started to beat on the couch pillows with her fist. She arched her back and screamed, "Aw, shit, Daddy! Daddy! Do me like that!" She cupped her right breast and squeezed it in her hand.

I continued to manipulate her until she began to shake. I felt that and began to flick her clit with my tongue, sucking and pulling on it. All the while my fingers continued their assault.

"Huh-uh! Huh-uh! Daddy! I'm done! I'm done, Daddy. Oh, Daddy!" she hollered, leaning over the couch and biting into the pillow.

I waited for her to finish, then opened her ass cheeks and licked around her back door, sucking and biting all over her globes before backing away with the taste of her pussy on my breath.

She jumped her thick ass up from the couch, with her fingers playing with her pussy lips. "Let me ride that dick now, Daddy. I need to feel you inside of me right now." She walked up on me and squeezed my dick, dropping down to her knees and taking my boxers with her. "Damn, Daddy, you seem like you ready for me already. I don't even need to suck it, do I?" she smiled, licking her lips and stroking my monster up and down.

I tilted my hips forward. "Stop playing wit' me. Fair exchange ain't no robbery, shorty. Handle that bidness."

She continued to stroke my dick up and down before popping the head into her mouth and sucking me halfway. She pulled back, leaving it sloppy wet, and slid back down, gagging a bit. When she pulled her mouth off, it was shiny with her spit. "Daddy, look how long it is tonight! Please let me ride this muthafucka. I can tell by all of these veins you're fien'ing for me just as bad." She sucked me back into her mouth and started to go crazy, slurping loudly and pumping him at the same time. She got to sucking so fast and firm I felt like I was getting ready to bust.

"Hold on, baby. Hold on." I got on my knees, and then my back. "Get you thick ass up here and ride this meat. Come on." I held my dick by the base, waiting for her.

She leaned over and kissed the head, then in a giddy-like fashion straddled my waist and fell forward until her breasts were against my chest. I could feel her hard nipples poking me. She reached under herself and found my pole. I held her ass wide open while she wiggled from right to left. The big head found her lips and slowly slipped inside her oven. It felt like as tight, wet and warm just like her mouth. She sank backward and engulfed me, and her eyes rolled into the back of her head before she sat up.

My eyes were super low. I could feel my dick jumping inside of her channel, excited and ready. I gripped that fat ass and held it. "Fuck you waiting on? Ride this big muthafucka!" I hollered, pulling her ass down on it.

"Uh!" She sank down the length of me until she was sitting on my ball. "Okay, Daddy. Damn, okay." She sounded out of breath.

She rolled her back and popped forward, then backward again. She picked up a steady rhythm, and before I could say another word she was riding me like a jockey. Her big titties hopped up and down on her chest and bounced into each other. Sweat trickled down the middle of them and onto her stomach.

I continued to hold her round ass in my big hands. "Fuck Daddy, baby. Ride this dick."

"I am. I am. I am. I am. Aw, shit. I am, Daddy!" She popped her hips harder and harder, causing her breasts to go haywire. The scent of our mingled sexes rose to my nose. I could feel my dick sliding deep into her hot womb while her juices oozed along my ass cheeks.

She started to bounce up and down on me like a bouncy house, digging her nails into my chest. "It's big, Daddy. It's big. But. But. I'm taking it. I'm taking it. Every time. I take this shit," she whimpered, riding me faster and faster.

There was nothing like a woman who knew how to ride my pipe. Thanks to my old man, I was blessed with more than eleven inches of penis. Most bitches acted like they were scared to try me out for size, but not Yani. I'd taken her virginity when she was sixteen years old, and even then she'd taken it like a champ. She always said it was because of me she couldn't fuck wit' niggas who had small pipes. She said they had to be at least eight inches or better. Even though I'd been tearing that pussy up since high school, her shit was always as tight as a fist. I never understood that, but I was thankful because a bad woman with a nice pussy was a rarity these days. Most females in Chicago lost their walls by the time they were fifteen. It was just the way it was. In this city, young females were preyed on by the older niggas in their thirties and forties. They took being a sugar daddy to a whole other level.

I grabbed Yani's hips and slammed her down on my dick as hard as I could. *Bam. Bam. Bam. Bam.* Her ass jiggled in my lap and her juices dripped onto the carpet.

"Yes. Yes. Yes. Yes. Daddy. Fuck me, Daddy. Fuck me. Aw. Daddy. Daddy. Aw, shit!" She sped up the pace and squeezed her eyelids together tightly. "I'm cummin', Daddy. I'm cummin'. I'm cumming!" She pressed her stomach on top of mine and got to twerking as hard as she could, sucking my dick with her pussy's walls.

It felt so good I couldn't hold back. I slid my finger into her asshole and ran it in and out. "Here Daddy cum. Here. Daddy. Cum!" I growled, busting and shooting up her womb.

I rolled her onto her back and licked the sweat from her neck, sucking all over it. "This my pussy, li'l momma. This pussy belong to Daddy. You my li'l one," I proclaimed, sucking all over her body.

***

I ran the loofa over the front of her breasts as she lay with her back against my chest in the tub. I had candles burning all around it and Trey Songz's *Jupiter Love* bellowing out of the speakers. I kissed the back of her neck.

"Daddy, you know I don't like you being in those streets like that. I'd prefer for you to keep handling your business with the barber shops and whatnot and just leave the slums alone altogether. But I been thinking." She raised her foot in the air. Her toenails were painted pink and the tips were white, like her fingernails. The water cascaded off her feet and poured back into the tub. Her toes were one of the sexiest things about her to me. In my opinion, there was nothing more sexy than a woman with pretty fingers and toes.

"What you been thinking, bae?" I slid my hand down her stomach and opened her sex lips, sliding my middle finger inside of her.

She placed her ankle on the rim of the tub, leaving her pussy wide open for me. "I was out in Riverdale yesterday, fucking around wit' my cousin KiKi that stay in the Gardens. Anyway, she was saying that fool Pesos been jacking about what he did to you and your old man. That nigga acting like he ain't gon' catch no flack behind all of that. It's insulting. But anyway, Daddy, I think you should get up wit' his punk-ass. We can't let what happened to you and Castro go un-avenged. Fuck that. My nigga is a savage."

I grunted. "You already know I ain't about to let that shit ride. I been getting my head together before I step back out into that jungle. My niggas been hitting me up, trying to see what's good. I ain't even responded to them." I pulled my fingers out of her pussy and sniffed them. I loved her scent. Pussy was one hell of a fragrance.

"Yeah, well, don't think I'm saying I want you

41

out there like that. I just want you to hit that nigga, and then get back to doing what you were doing before all of this crap happened. I don't like hearing about nigga's jacking on your name. I feel personally offended. If I have to, I'll bust my gun for you, too. You already know that. Don't you?" She turned around to look into my face, searchingly.

I smiled. "Yeah, I know you'd handle your business if it came down to it. But I got this shit. I ain't losing no sleep over that fuck-nigga. I want him to keep on thinking it's sweet."

Even though I was downplaying it to her, I was feeling like a straight sucka, for real. Not only had Pesos killed my father and popped me up, but now he was jacking on me. In Chicago, when a nigga got down on a homie and he didn't do shit about it, that word got around fast. Before a homie knew it, every jack-boy would be at his head thinking they could lay him down and no consequences would come from it. He'd also lose the respect of the hood. The females would take pity on him, but at the same time they wouldn't fuck wit' him because he'd be considered soft and a target. Didn't no woman wanna fuck with a soft man who couldn't protect her.

So, hell yeah, I was feeling some type of way. I was heated, feeling sick and emasculated. But I didn't feel I could let Yani know that. I could only let her see what was going to happen in time. I had plans for Pesos' bitch-ass. I also needed to get my money all the way up so I could fulfill my promise to my father in regards to buying my mother her own church. I had a lot on my plate. It was up to me to master my struggles.

"Daddy, just be careful. He got all of them niggas out there following behind his ass like he's some sort of king or something. KiKi said he wouldn't be half the man he was if his brother had not left all of that power to him before he got indicted. No matter what, though, I know he don't know who he's fucking with. But he'll find out real fast."

She shrieked. "Damn, what's making you get so hard?" she asked, bumping the crack of her booty up against the length of my pole.

I shook my head and cupped her titties. "I just like when you talk like you know what type of nigga you got. You already know this nigga finna feel my pain." I sucked her earlobe and lifted her up a little, leaned back, and slid her down on my dick again. Even under the water her pussy was nice and hot. I held her waist and got to bouncing her up and down, swishing the water around in the tub.

"Kill him, Daddy. Kill him. I'ma. I'm. I'ma. Have. Kiki. Aw, shit. Put you up. On Game. Fuck me harder!"

Hood Rich

Chapter 4

I had a right-hand man by the name of Brat. I called her my right-hand man because even though she was a female, she ain't act like one under most circumstances. Brat was 5'6" tall and about 160 pounds. She had a real pretty face with a long scar on the left side that she'd gotten because two females had jumped her when we were in the eighth grade. I was talking to one of the chicks and she got jealous of the relationship I had with Brat. She thought more was going on between us than actually was.

Even though Brat was a female, she and I had never come at each other on no sexual shit. She was like my actual nigga. I wasn't attracted to her like that, at least not on that level. So, when I found out the female I was talking to back then had used a box cutter to slice the side of her face, I nearly broke my neck getting to the hospital. But she told her people to not let me pass. She told them she didn't want to see me ever again, and that broke my heart. Brat was the first female I ever loved outside of my mother and sister.

She didn't fuck wit' me on no level until our tenth grade year. That's when a few of the oppositions were planning to gun me down in my car after school one day. She begged me to leave early, and I did.

I guess they figured since they couldn't catch up with me, they'd holler at one of my homies from back then. They wound up shooting him twenty times a block away from the school. He could have been me had it not been for Brat. So, I'd felt indebted to her ever since then.

On the 23rd day of my mourning over my old man, Brat showed up at my crib just as I was pulling the blanket over Yani's body. I'd just dicked her down for two hours straight, and even I was tired. I had plans on getting me at least eight hours of sleep when Brat rang the doorbell and sent me a text telling me to answer the door.

I pulled it open and she looked me up and down before stepping past me. She had her red-and-black Chevy Astro van sitting in front of my crib, banging that Cardi B. *Drip, Drip.*

"Nigga, I can't believe you ain't got up wit' me yet. I know we finna go and holler at these niggas, right?" She lifted her shirt to show me she was carrying two chrome .45s with pearl handles. "I got the low-down on where that nigga Pesos lay his head. I say we roll through that bitch and lay him down. Cut his nuts off before we put two in his head. You feeling me?" she asked as her phone vibrated. She looked at the face and hit ignore. She was dressed in a black-and-red Marc Jacobs fit with a Chicago Bulls fitted cap and retro #8 Jordans. She had three gold links around her neck and a pink-and-gold Rolex on her left wrist.

"You saying you know where he lay his head at, for sure? Like right now-type shit?" I asked, getting geeked up. I felt like killing up some shit, especially after all the things Yani had told me.

"Hell yeah. He got a baby by one of my li'l hos,

but he been dogging her out like crazy. A few days ago he beat her so bad she had to spend a night in the hospital. He one of them type of niggas." She frowned and walked into the kitchen, opening my refrigerator and taking out one of my Mr. Pure Apple Juices. She opened the top and came back into the living room. "We can't honor them bitch-niggas flexing on us like that. They took yo' old man, put slugs in your body, and we ain't did shit yet? They're already the opposition. We don't fuck wit' them blue guys, no way. It's drip-drip all day, everyday." She turned around to show me the red flag hanging from her right pocket. "I got, like, four of the homies in the van right now, ready to ride down these niggas on some killing-shit. All you gotta say is the word, and we'll leave red rags all over that nigga's house, along with his head. That's on my blood, Heinous."

She was getting me geeked up. I was tired as hell from fucking Yani, but she was giving me some added strength. "Jo, let's ride out. If you know where this nigga sleeping, then let's go before he wake the fuck up. I feel like killing something. Anything."

I made my way into my back room where Yani was lying in the bed, already snoring. Somehow she'd thrown the blanket off and her legs were wide open. I planted a juicy kiss right on her pussy lips, sucking them into my mouth before steppin' back and smiling.

"Damn, she strapped." Brat shook her head from the doorway. "I always wanted to know what that was like." She grabbed her crotch as if she had a penis and bit her bottom lip.

"Damn, nigga. Take yo' ass back to the front of the crib. Quit jocking my bitch. I'll be ready in a minute." I pushed her ass out of the door and closed it.

Yani moved around in the bed before opening her eyes. She stretched her arms above her head. "Where you finna go, bae?"

"Nowhere. I got some shit I'm about to take care of. You can stay sleep. I should be back in a few hours." I stuffed my .40 Glock into my Ferragamo jeans and slid my arms through the holes in the Kevlar vest before sliding my black and gray fatigues over it. I threw on a pair of black Jordans, too, just in case I had to run or some shit.

Yani, jumped out of the bed naked and wrapped her arms around my neck. "Daddy, please be careful. I know you can hold your own and all of that shit, but I'm scared for you. Please be smart. I don't know what I would do without you."

I hugged her and kissed her forehead. "I love you, ma. I got this. Don't worry about me. You just get you some sleep so when I come back we can go another round." I squeezed that fat ass and cupped it underneath. I could feel the slight wrinkles of her kitty lips on my knuckles.

"I love you, too, Daddy. But you know I ain't about to get no sleep wit' you in these streets like that."

***

48

"Fuck them hand guns, Heinous. You gotta fuck with this Mach .90. This bitch spit eighty rounds, and it's accurate as you gon' get when it comes to rapid firing. Huh, you can hold this down. I'ma use this other one," Capo said, handing the Mach .90 to me.

I was seated in the back of the Astro van in a bucket seat, Li'l Wayne's *Gotti* banging out of the speakers. I was two blunts in on some Chicago Kush and had popped two Mollies. I was ready to kill up some shit with no mercy. "Good looking, Jo. This bitch feel a li'l heavy, too." I popped the long clip out and looked it over. It had holes on the side of it where I could see the metallic bullets lined up vertically within it.

Brat handed me the blunt over her shoulder. She was behind the wheel of the van with her red rag around her neck. "Keep this Kush in yo' system, Heinous. I had to smoke a couple niggas after the club a few days ago because they were pulling and feeling all over my main bitch on the dance floor. I tried to holler at the niggas on some civil shit inside the club, but that didn't work. Got to calling me all kinds of dyke bitches and shit. Flung my li'l ho on the ground, and you know I couldn't have that. Long story short, while I was smoking them niggas, this Kush made that shit look like a movie. I could actually see the bullets going into them and busting their flesh wide open. It was cool as hell."

I took the blunt and took five strong pulls from it, inhaling and feeling the smoke burning my lungs. "I been blowing on this shit for a month straight now. I know what it do. This was my Pop's favorite shit." I felt a twinge of sorrow go through me.

Brat looked into the mirror. "Damn, I forgot I ordered this pound from your old head. That's fucked up, bruh. I miss Castro."

"That's why we gotta bring heat to these niggas. I don't give a fuck who out here. I'm letting this bitch ride until it's empty." Capo cocked the Mach and smiled while looking at it. "Let me hit that Kush, Blood."

I handed it back to him and checked my phone. Yani had already sent me two texts saying she loved me and to be careful. I didn't know why it was so hard for me to settle down and just be with her on some one-on-one shit. She really was a good woman. In Chicago, a good woman was so hard to find. Everybody had hidden agendas here. The city was so fucked up that our motto was if a nigga can't be used, then he's useless. Ever since Yani and I had been a part of each other's lives, she'd always been able to hold her own on all levels. She was more of an asset to me than anything else. Even though my heart, for the most part, was a cold atmosphere, for her there was a lot of unconditional love in it.

"Heinous, I ain't been able to get in touch with KiKi just yet, so we gon' roll through this bitch and spray they ass down. Hit whoever out there. Then, once we get addresses for Pesos and shit, we'll make a house call and really cause some damage."

She pulled into an alley on 144th and Normal,

50

right behind a black van with rust spots all over it. She turned off her ignition and pulled her rag all the way over her face, took her gloves out of her pockets, and slid them on.

I was doing the same thing. I slid the red ski mask over my face along with the red leather gloves, took the Mach, and cocked it. "I thought we was about to hit this nigga crib tonight. You telling me we just on some drive-by shit?" I asked, disappointed. I wanted to lay my head on my pillow tonight knowing that nigga Pesos was deceased.

"Yeah, well, we gotta shake some shit up. Soon as we spray they ass down, them niggas gon' run and regroup. Once they do that, we'll catch his ass slipping at home while he's plotting on his next move. That's how shit goes. You already know that."

I shrugged my shoulders. "Fuck it. Let's just go and handle this business. I just need to kill up some niggas from this hood, anyway. They put so many slugs into my pops' shit that it ain't no way that fool did it by his self. He got a lot of help, so if we don't see him, let's murder the help." I scrunched my face and jumped out of that van, and then got set up in the other one. I waited until the other three gunners who were with us got inside of it before I jumped in as well.

"One of you niggas come and drive. I wanna hit up some of these dudes, too," Brat demanded, fixing her mask on her face. She came and knelt beside me. "You ready to do this shit? Make these niggas pay for what they did to you. It's drip-drip time."

"I'ma show you better than I can tell you." I got situated by the door, ready to slid it back when the time was right.

Our van circled around South Lanbley, then Corliss and over to St. Lawrence. These streets made up the perimeter of the Aldgeld Gardens. The streets looked deserted with only a few people out. Most were women and children. I didn't give a fuck how mad I was and ready to avenge my father's death, I wasn't feeling just killing up a bunch of women and children to make a statement. I wanted to eat at the flesh of the niggas who'd shot me and my Pops.

"Fuck these niggas at? Ain't shit but a bunch of shorties and mothers out here." I continued to look around, hoping I could find a group of dudes, but was unable to locate any sight like that.

"Blood, pull this bitch down the street to Golden Gate. KiKi said Pesos and his crew love playing basketball at night. It's about six o'clock. I wouldn't doubt all of them niggas are over there on that type of shit."

I was hoping they were. My trigger finger was itching like it had a rash on it. I wanted to see a nigga's brains leaking out of his skull. I was high, and them Mollies had me wired. I was in a zone and thirsty for death.

Our driver made a right onto East 130th and South Eberhart. That was where Golden Gate Park was located. As soon as we turned the corner, I could see a bunch of dudes on the basketball courts. They looked to be about a hundred deep. They were lined up along the gate, some watching the game and others looking toward the street where we were set to drive down. I guessed they were on security. Most of them had their hands on their waists and mugs on their faces. Blue rags hung from their back pockets.

Brat tapped my shoulder. "There go Pesos and his crew, right over there." Her voice sounded giddy.

For a second I blanked out. I could feel the bullets entering my body while me and my father sat idly in the parking lot of the Gardens. I remembered the side of my father's face exploding, his warm blood drenching me after the windows shattered into my lap. Suddenly the sight of Pesos and all of his homies was causing me to shake a little bit, as if I was reliving what they'd done to myself and my old man. I felt myself getting angry.

I looked over to the court and saw Pesos standing on the sidelines by the bleachers with his fitted cap's brim turned to the right slide at a hard 90-degree angle. He had a blue bandana around his neck. He was shirtless with two guns on his hips, one on each side. He stood just off the basketball courts. Behind him were about fifty dudes. All of them had blue rags around their necks and guns on their hips as far as I could see.

I nodded my head. "Let's wet these fuck-niggas, Blood. Bitch-ass niggas think it's sweet."

Brat bounced her head up and down. "That's what the fuck I'm talking about. Let's make a movie, Blood. When 'you turn that corner, Heinous, you slide that door back, and me, you, and Capo gon' let these Machs holler. No mercy." Brat cocked her Mach.

I looked over and saw there was also a bunch of teenagers in the park looking on as spectators. "Make sure y'all try and stay away from them kids. It's about ten of they li'l asses out there. We ain't trying to kill no innocent shorties." I placed my hand on the door handle.

"Man, fuck them li'l niggas. The way I see it, they our future oppositions. Might as well exterminate they asses right the fuck now, that way we ain't gotta deal with them later," Brat laughed, getting down on her knee beside me.

I guess she had a point, for the most part. I mean, there were a lot of kids about the age of thirteen and fourteen doing a nice amount of the killings in Chicago. You couldn't underestimate nobody. Not kids. Not women. Not old folks. Everybody was a threat in my book. It didn't take much to pull a trigger.

"Well, fuck it, let's go. Blood. circled around again, then bend this corner right here on 130th. Once you do that, you gon' speed up and stop right in front of the basketball court. We'll take it from there." I looked up at him and pulled my red rag all the way over my face.

I could feel my heart pounding in my chest as we rolled past the park the first time. I peeked and saw most of the dudes who were out there were armed. I wasn't expecting us to take a lot of shots to the van, but I was prepared. I had to seek my revenge on

Pesos and let that nigga know it wasn't sweet, along with my city. Word was already out about what he did to me and my pops, and it was only a matter of time before cats started robbing my barbershops, thinking it sweet. I couldn't have that. I had to set the precedent right away.

Our driver circled around and was back at the corner where we started. "Awright, Blood, here we go. Guns ready." He hit the corner and stepped on the gas. My heart got to pounding in my chest. This was it. It was time to put up or shut up.

When the van slammed on its brakes, I wound up crashing into Brat before I regained my footing and pulled the side door open. Brat placed her shoulder against mine and let her Mach ride at the same time I did.

"Rest in peace, Pesos." *Bocka. Bocka. Bocka. Bocka. Bocka. Bocka. Bocka. Bocka. Bocka.*

The Mach jumped in my hand again and again. Shells spit into the interior of the van and rolled along the shag carpet. Fire spit out of the barrel. I watched my bullets spit into the crowd, and people got to dropping to the pavement, leaking. The crowd disbursed, and the people inside it who were not yet hit got to running in every direction. I could hear screams and groans alongside our gunshots.

Pesos ran for a second, then turned around in the middle of the basketball court, upped two .44 Desert Eagles, and got to busting back at us. *Boom. Boom. Boom. Boom. Boom.* His bullets slammed into our van, rocking it side-to-side. He continued to shoot as if he had a death wish.

I closed the door back for a second until his shots stopped, then opened it again, aimed at him, and started to buck again. *Bocka. Bocka. Bocka. Bocka. Bocka.* He ran a little more and jumped behind the metal bleachers.

Brat continued to buck her Mach with her red rag over her face. She held it with two hands. Shells popped out of it and onto the curb. Smoke rose from the back of it and lingered in the air. The heavy scent of gunpowder and hot metal was in the air.

"Bitch-ass niggas. Fuck, I'm out!" she yelled and jumped back into the van. "Empty that clip, Heinous, and let's go."

I sent ten more shots in the direction of Pesos and watched a few of them ricochet off the bleachers in bright sparks before my gun was empty. It jerked in my hand, spitting out the last bullet. "A'ight, let's roll," I hollered to our driver.

He stepped on the gas. The van took off from the curb.

Capo opened the very back door of the van and started to fire at Pesos' men as we drove away from the scene. Somehow they had recovered and were rocking our van with bullet after bullet. I was ducked down, praying I didn't get hit with another slug. I wasn't trying to feel that heat. We needed to get the fuck out of there and to safety.

When we came to the corner of South Maryland, four dudes ran into the middle of the streets with Techs in their hands and got to chopping at us. *Thaa-*

at! Thaa-at! Thaa-at! Thaa-at! Eight big bullet holes appeared in the windshield of the van before it shattered. Our driver ducked down and stepped on the gas to plow through them. They jumped out of the way only to keep on spraying, knocking out all of the windows.

"Get the fuck out of here!" I hollered, fearing the worst. I was thinking the same thing that happened to me and my father was going to happen to us. I was praying the van's tires weren't shot out. We were a long way from home and in Pesos' territory. I was sure we had no chance of making it out of his jungle.

Our driver stepped on the gas and shot out into the busy intersection, crashing into the back of a busted-up station wagon that was missing a muffler. *Wham!* The van wound up in the middle of the intersection on the grass median. Luckily, our driver kept the wheel. He made a U-turn on the grass as more and more shots rocked the van's exterior. He hopped off of the median and was able to make it down the busy street with a bunch of cars blowing their horns at us.

I looked out our back window and saw the station wagon catch fire, Before we made a right six blocks up, the station wagon was engulfed in flames.

Hood Rich

Chapter 5

Three days later my mother summoned me to her crib out in Evanston. She'd just gotten back from Detroit where she'd been on a seven-day retreat.

She came from the back of the house and dropped a duffle bag at my feet. "Is this the reason they killed your father, Jahrome?" she asked, looking down on me. My mother was the only person who called me by my first name. Anytime anyone else tried to call me by it, I snapped on them immediately. I'd never liked my first name.

I shrugged my shoulders. "I don't know. What's in there?" I sat up on the couch, then knelt down and unzipped the bag. I looked inside at the contents.

"You know what's in there, Jahrome. Don't think I'm stupid and didn't know what was going on with you and your father, because I'm not, and I did. Now, explain to me if this is the reason my husband was murdered?" She sat down on the loveseat across from me.

I moved my hand around the duffle bag, and counted ten bricks of what I assumed to be heroin. They were packaged in tin foil with red Chinese writing on them and wrapped multiple times in saran wrap. I was accustomed to our kilos of China White heroin coming just like that. My old man had a plus with a few of the Asians in China Town. Before he passed away, he'd been getting kilos of heroin from them at a price of thirteen thousand apiece.

I nodded my head at my mother. "Yeah, Ma.

Them dudes was trying to get us to just hand over our work, but Pops wasn't going. I wanted to leave way before anything like that transpired, but Pops insisted he knew how to do business with those clowns, so we stayed. And you already know what happened from there." I zipped the bag back and looked over at her. I had another lump in my throat. I was feeling real sick over my old man again. I hoping my mother didn't break down or nothing. I knew I wasn't strong enough to witness that again.

She lowered her head and clasped her hands together. "Ever since me and your father have been together, I've been trying to pull him from the darkness of those streets, but they have always had a strong hold on him. I never understood why because I've never been the type of woman who wanted to live the flashy life. I am content with the small things. I know God blesses those who remain faithful to him. John 10:10 says our Father came so that we may have life, but not just a regular life, but one of abundance. All your father had to do was submit to the Lord, and everything he was in those streets hustling for would have been rendered unto him through Jehovah's bounties. But, because he wouldn't listen to me, I am without a husband and my children are without their father. Nobody wins when you play in the Devil's casino of life. He is the house, and the house always wins. It's that simple, son." She sighed. "I counted ten of those things in there. I pulled them from the truck on the night of his murder. There are another five in the safe in the bedroom. That's fifteen. What are they worth altogether?" she looked over at me.

I shrugged my shoulders. "I could make fifteen thousand off of each kilo. That's a hundred and fifty thousand, easily." I avoided eye contact with her. I didn't know where she was going with things. My mother had a way of asking questions to reveal a person's true nature and intentions. Everything she was asking me had a purpose. I was sure of it.

"And do you not think your father's life was worth more than one point two million dollars, son?"

I shook my head. "Yeah, Ma, of course it is. I wasn't saying it like that. I was just letting you know what they were worth on the street."

She stared at me for a long time, then her eyes got watery. "And I suppose you want me to give you this poison so you can pick up where he left off, huh? I mean, after all, it's over a million dollars to be made. Why shouldn't I? Right?"

"Ma, I loved my father, and still do. But he's gone. He died over this dope. What are we supposed to do with it?"

"I'ma tell you what I'ma do with it. I'ma flush this poison down the toilet." She shot from the couch and grabbed the bag, rushing to the bathroom in the back of the house.

I jumped up in hot pursuit. "Ma, wait. Hold up." I rushed to catch up with her. I wasn't about to let her flush a million plus dollars down the toilet. That would be stupid, I felt.

I don't know where she'd gotten the knife, but when I got to the bathroom she'd stabbed one of the kilos of heroin directly in the center and sliced a long gash inside of it. Then she held it over the toilet and began to shake the contents out of it. A billow of heroin powder wafted into the air like a white cloud.

"Mama, what are you doing? That's eighty thousand dollars right there!" I tried to hold my breath, but I had already inhaled some of the cloud. I could taste it on my tongue. It burned my throat and nostrils at the same time.

"I don't care about no freaking money, Jahrome. This dope killed your father. I won't let it be the cause of your death, as well. I'd rather die first!" she yelled before coughing with her tongue hanging out of her mouth.

The heroin was all over the bathroom floor and toilet. She had some of it on her dress, face, and hair. It looked like flour. She dumped as much of the contents into the toilet as she could and flushed it, then grabbed another one, getting ready to stab it.

My head was spinning. I felt dizzy, and it was like my hearing intensified. I could actually hear her breath coming out of her lungs and the lids of her eyes every time she blinked. My heart was pounding. I felt like I was having an out-of-body experience. I dropped to my knees and looked over at my mother.

Instead of dumping the second kilo of dope into the toilet, she was seated with her back up against the wall, the kilo on her lap. Her eyes were low. She ran her hand over her face, still covered in dope, and shook her head. Her tongue ran over her lips. "What is happening to me, Jahrome? I feel like I'm having a heart attack. I can't feel my face."

I sat on my ass and scooted over to her. Dope continued to rain down in a puffy cloud from the air. I could smell the China White all in my nose. My eyes were burning, yet at the same time I felt pain-free and happy. I didn't understand the happy part because our situation was so fucked up, but as hard as I tried to be angry about it, the dope wouldn't let me. "Mama, we gotta get you to a hospital. This heroin is in your system. I don't think your body can handle it. Come on, let me help you up." I reached for her hand.

She yanked it away from me. She jammed the knife into the second kilo and opened it. "Nall, you just wanna get me out of the way so you can take this blood-dope and sell it. I'm not as stupid as you think, Jahrome. I have to get rid of all of it. It belongs to the devil, and the devil will not have my family. Not today, not ever. He's a liar and the father of all lies. I rebuke these drugs in the mighty name of Jesus, and you too, son."

She waved the kilo wildly over the toilet, dumping it out. Once again a cloud of powder rose into the air and covered the bathroom. It was so strong I started to choke, and she did as well.

My father had said time and time again he'd gotten the best heroin in Chicago from a Chinese woman by the name of Mama Kim. I remembered him bragging that all her kilos were 95% pure, which was as strong as a dealer could possibly get it.

I was so high watching my mother that I couldn't

move. My eyelids were heavy and my whole body was tingling like crazy. I didn't have any more fight in me. I just wanted to chill and let the high run its course. I felt like I'd popped ten Oxycodone, and drank a bottle of lean. I was lifted. "Ma, okay, you can do whatever you want with that dope. I ain't gon' fight you on it, but we gotta get out of here."

She sat back on her legs and ran her hand over her face again. Then she held her hand out in front of her and looked at it as if it was an alien. She dropped the half-emptied kilo and sat on her bottom. "Son, I think I'm high. I hear this music in my head, and everything looks weird I just want to close my eyes." She crawled over to me and laid her head on my chest. She closed her eyes, and I could hear her breathing heavily.

I wiggled from under her and stood up, staggering on my feet. I grabbed her under the arms before picking her up and carrying her out of the bathroom. My mother wasn't a big woman. She was about 5'5" tall and weighed about 150 pounds. I carried her into her bedroom and laid her on the bed. She scooted backward until her head was on the pillow. There was heroin all over her face, along with tears. As they came down her cheeks, they turned the dope a yellowish color.

I got ready to leave the room so I could go and clean up the mess. I staggered on my feet and bumped into her dresser, knocking her phone onto the floor. I bent over to pick it up and fell on my ass. I wound up with my head against the dresser while I nodded for a few minutes. Drool came out of the corner of my mouth.

"Jahrome! Jahrome! Baby, where are you? I can't breathe!" my mother yelled and kicked her feet on the big bed.

I jumped up and rushed to her side, got onto the bed and crawling across it on my knees. It felt like I was getting higher and higher. I was seeing two of everything. The music in my head was so loud I could barely think straight. My body kept on wanting to drift to the left. My equilibrium must've been thrown off. "I'm here, Mama. I'm here."

She reached out for me and pulled me down in her arms, wrapping them around my neck. "I'm scared, baby. I keep seeing your father. My heart is killing me, and I can't breathe. Hold me for a little while, at least until this feeling...." Her eyelids slowly closed. She started to snore with her mouth wide open.

I lay my forehead again hers with my eyes closed. I felt so weak and like I could feel my blood flowing through me. There was a pounding in my chest that felt like an 808 drum. Every time my heart beat, it caused the back of my eyes to throb.

"I miss him so much, Jahrome. I told him not to go out that night. He should have...." Once again she nodded out and began to snore. She was asleep for about a minute, then jerked and woke up. "Had he listened to me, he'd still be alive. What am I going to do, baby?" She hugged me tighter and wrapped her legs around me.

I lay there with my eyes closed, feeling the effect the drug had on my system. I was gone in the head, higher than I had ever been before in my life. I could hear my mother snoring under me. Her nails dug into my back. I tried my best to keep my eyes open, but the battle was lost no more than three minutes after she'd passed out.

***

When I awoke, it was three hours later. I opened my eyes to find my mother standing in the center of the bedroom in just her panties and no bra. She had her head tilted sideways, tooting a line of heroin from the top of her dresser. She held her phone in one hand. After she tooted the line, she held her head backward, and pinched her nostril.

I was still disoriented. I shook my head, jumped out of the bed, and made my way over to her "What the fuck are you doing?"

She jumped and dropped her phone on the floor. There was a white boy on the screen teaching the viewers how to snort dope. I saw she was on YouTube.

"Baby, I'm sorry, but I can't take this pain. Me sniffing this stuff has been the only escape I've had from the reality of your father's murder. It's like I feel closer to him, and I can't feel any pain. I need this stuff. Maybe God had him leave it behind for me to cope." She licked her lips and closed her eyes again, leaning against her dresser. Her elbow landed in the heroin, but it seemed as if she didn't notice.

My head was pounding horribly. I felt like I was about to throw up. My ribs were even cramping on me. I opened my eyes wide to try to shake off the effects of the drug. I grabbed her by the shoulders and shook her. "Are you out of your fucking mind? Huh? Do you know what that dope'll do to you? Think, Ma."

She shook her head. "I don't want to think right now, baby. I've been thinking and doing the right thing my whole life, and where has it gotten me? Huh? Your father is dead, we're in debt, and I still don't have my church I've worked so hard to obtain. Life just isn't fair. It hurts all the time. Since your father's death, the only time I've been without pain in when this stuff has been in my system. I can't take anymore agony, son. I'm at my breaking point."

My mind was blown because I couldn't wrap my head around the fact my mother wasn't smarter than this. She had to know heroin was a death sentence, that nothing good could come from her doing it. In fact, her father had died from an overdose of heroin in the early eighties. Three weeks later, her mother died from the same drug. So it wasn't like she was ignorant or naive to the drug. She had to know its long-term effects.

I was so taken aback I didn't know what to say. All I could do was stare at her in disbelief.

"Aw, don't look at me like that. You're no better than me. You could have saved your father's life, but you didn't. You share a part of the blame." She broke into a fit of tears and pointed at her room door. "Just get out of my face, Jahrome! I don't need another person judging me. 'Judge not lest ye be judged.' That's what the word says." She closed her eyes and smiled, then lowered her head and shook it. "Just go, Jahrome. Leave my damn house. I'm lost right now!" She stepped in front of the dresser and looked down at its contents.

"Ma, you not about to get addicted to this shit. What is the matter with you?" I brushed all of the dope from the dresser, sending the pile onto the carpet. Some of it landed on top of her phone, covering the screen.

"What is your problem?" she screamed and ran at me with her fists balled up. "Get out of my house, Jahrome. Get out. Get out. Now!" She swung her arms like a windmill. Her punches connected with my head, shoulders, and the side of my neck.

I held up my guards then pushed her on the bed. She landed on her back, bounced up, and ran at me again, swinging wildly. "Get out. Get out. You're the reason my husband is dead. You did this. You did this. It should have been you and not him. It ain't fair. It just ain't fair."

I picked her up and tossed her on the bed again, this time all the way in the middle. I grabbed the duffle bag that had the rest of the kilos in it from the floor and made my way out of her house. On the way out, I could hear her crying in the background.

I felt feeling worse than I ever had in my entire life.

Chapter 6

After going through that night with my mother, I felt like I was fucked up in the head. I honestly thought she felt I was responsible for my father's death and she would never look at me the same way ever again. That hurt my heart because I knew I'd done everything in my power to get my old man to pull away from the Gardens before the shooting occurred. But he hadn't listened to me.

I felt guilty and upset at the world. Even watching the news and seeing we'd killed nine people the night we attacked Pesos and his crew couldn't make me feel better, especially since none of the faces the media outlet had posted belonged to Pesos. I was sick and felt like I'd sunken into a dark place. The night after I came from my mother's house, I stayed up for four hours tooting the China White, trying to get as far away from my sorrows as possible. I felt like in one month I'd lost my father and my mother. It was almost enough to make me lose myself.

***

Three days later I sat at the long table with a bunch of Bloods around me. Brat sat to my right, and Capo sat to my left. On each side of us were other Bloods from our crew who we ran with from time to time. See, in Chicago a nigga had to be plugged with one crew or another. It was impossible for any man to walk the streets of the city without gang

69

protection. Every block in the slums belonged to a crew. If a nigga was not a part of that crew or his crew had not made a treaty with the crew who ran that block and they caught him slipping, nine times out of ten a nigga was a dead man. And the streets didn't care whether a nigga was male or female. They blew heads off for being out-of-bounds just the same.

So even though I wasn't with following no man other than God, I rolled with a bunch of Blood Stones who operated out of an area in Chicago called Moe Town. We ran under the red rag and the five-point star. Our rivals were all blue crews, and even some who were gold. Our branch of monsters were made up of cold-blooded killers who lived to cause funerals and get money by any means.

Me, I was my own man. I was never the type to kill just because. There had to be a purpose, a method to my madness. Sometimes I found myself in jams because of the niggas and bitches I rolled with, though.

Lost Boy was the so-called leader of our crew. Our headquarters were set up in an apartment building on 53rd and Green. Lost Boy insisted we all meet up to have a group meeting every Friday, without excuse. This particular Friday he stormed into the apartment building and slammed the door so loud I jumped and upped two of my pistols, aiming them at the door. Brat had done the same thing. I had red rags around the handles to help with my grip. It also helped my pistols look good to me.

Lost Boy was 6'6" tall and weighed about 350

pounds. He was huge and black as the night's sky without stars shining in it. His eyes were always red. He had tattoos all over his face and bald head with five-point stars up and down his black arms.

"Jo, sit y'all asses down and put them punk-ass guns away. On my Blood, I got a bone to pick with all of you niggas today." He wiped his mouth with his right hand and looked all around the room.

I slowly sat back in my chair after fixing the hammers on my guns. I slid them back into my waistband and mugged him. We locked eyes, and he curled his upper lip.

"Fuck you looking at me like that for, Heinous? You got something to say?" Two of his security Bloods came and stood behind him. All three of them mugged me with anger. I could sense the tension in the room and it made me uncomfortable, but I wasn't afraid of these niggas. I had grown up with them. I knew they were killers, but that didn't spook me because I was one, too. I had just as many bodies under my belt as they did, if not more.

Brat leaned into my ear. "Come on, Heinous. Don't start no shit wit' Lost Boy today. Let's just hear him out and get up out of here. You feel me? We got shit to do."

"Well, li'l nigga, you got something to say?"

I felt like this nigga was trying to antagonize me. I didn't like nobody poking at me. I didn't give a fuck what position they held, I was still a man, and I demanded respect. I frowned. "Bruh, why you always gotta come to this meetings like you mad about something? That shit getting old." I was irritated and tired of his rhetoric. I felt like his thing was to shake up the crew before he gave his speech every week. I was sick of that bullshit, and I just couldn't bite my tongue.

Brat lowered her head and shook it. "Here we go with this shit."

Lost Boy nodded his head and placed both of his hands on the table. The apartment was just big enough to hold the four picnic tables that had been pushed together. They ran into the front and living room. All four had a red-and-black tablecloth draped over the top of them, so I really couldn't see where one table ended or the other began. They were always uncomfortable to sit on, though.

Lost Boy lowered his eyes and turned his face to the side, mugging me. "Every week yo' li'l ass got something to say. That's what I'm getting tired of." He sucked his teeth. "In case you didn't notice, I'm the one that run this shit, not you. Muthafuckas get together every Friday to hear me speak and pay me dues. Not the other way around. You understand that, li'l nigga?"

"I get all that shit, but I ain't finna be a part of nothing that don't let me speak what I'm feeling and thinking. Ain't no nigga walking this green earth got that kind of power over me, and never will. Now, I said what I said, and that's how I feel."

Both of his Blood guards pulled guns from the smalls of their backs and aimed them at me without saying a word. I watched both of them cock their hammers.

Brat jumped up with her guns out. "Hold on, niggas. Y'all ain't finna get down on my mans like that. We all about to die in this bitch. On the five," she promised.

Capo turned his face into an angry ball and upped his Mach .90, aiming it at Lost Boy's bodyguards. "We either family or not." He cocked it and pulled his red rag over his face so far upward I could only see his gray eyes.

Lost Boy continued to mug me. He waved his Blood guards off. "Y'all put that shit away. We ain't on that right now. It's good. Me and Heinous just having a li'l discussion, that's all. Ain't that right, Heinous?"

I had both guns on my lap with the hammers cocked under the table. I was high as fuck and wanted more than anything to knock his head loose. I had never liked Lost Boy. One of the reasons was because I'd been riding under the gang for five years and had never seen him put in any work. I didn't know if he was a killer or not. I knew his Blood guards were, but as far as he went, I just didn't know.

"Yeah, it's good, people. We just having a li'l discussion." I looked him in the eyes the entire time. I could see the hate in his eyes. It made me want to buck his ass even more. The city of Chicago forced niggas to be a part of families they didn't trust or like. In order to survive, a nigga either had to roll with them or be rolled over by another crew looking for loose prey.

He snickered and stood back from the table. "Awright, the first order of business is the Altgeld Gardens. I just got word one of our vans was spotted out that was a few days ago when all of those people were killed at Golden Gate Park. Rumor has it their murders were in retaliation for your father's killing, Heinous. Is there something you wanna tell me?" he asked, looking into my eyes.

"Fuck them niggas out there. If it was up to me, I would have smoked every last one of them bitches. You can tell whoever told you about what happened that they can kiss my ass. Muthafuckas gon' pay for what they did to my old man. That's just that. I don't give a fuck what nobody say. Blame all that shit on me." I clenched my jaw and felt my heart pounding in my chest. I kept hearing my mother yelling that my father's murder was my fault. She said it should've been me and not him. I watched her toot the heroin up her nose, her breasts exposed on her chest. I shook my head and got to breathing so hard I became lightheaded.

"I get what you're saying, Heinous, but you already know how this shit goes. You niggas are my Bloods. Y'all don't do shit without my approval, because when you do, you make it to where every mob in Chicago that is aligned with Pesos and his crew want to go at our heads. Then I'm left in the dark. What if one of them would have tried to kill me while we were at our chiefs' meeting yesterday? Then what? Our gang would have been without a leader. With no guidance, all of your heads would be cut off."

"You heard about what happened to my pops and you ain't say shit, nigga. If something would have happened to anybody in your family, you would've had us kicking in doors, murdering shit on your behalf. But since it wasn't your old man, and it was mines, you ain't called an order yet. So I took shit into my own hands. I ain't done, either. I don't give a fuck about how you or nobody else feel about it. I lost my fucking pops!" I stood up with my chest heaving up and down.

Lost Boy flared his nostrils. "Heinous, sit yo' ass down, bruh. You testing my patience right now. I'm trying to be as sympathetic as I can, but you working my nerves."

I continued to hear my mother's voice in my head, blaming me for my father's murder. It was becoming too much. I began to wonder if she was right, and if she'd ever love me again. I needed to kill something or be killed to stop the pain that was beating deep inside of my heart. Something had to make it stop. I had both guns in my hands. "Fuck yo' patience. Do what you gotta do. Fuck you waiting on?"

He upped his Glock .9 and turned his face into a scowl. "You li'l bitch-ass nigga, you think I'm playing with you? I run this bitch, not yo' pretty-boy ass. Now sit the fuck down or I'm finna smoke you right here and right now." He cocked his pistol back.

Everybody at the table stood up, and most of them took a step away from the table. They huddled in the middle of the living room, looking from what they figured was a safe distance away from the action.

Brat had both of her guns out. "Lost Boy, we all family here, but if you hit my nigga, I swear on my life I'm gon' empty this whole clip in yo' ass, homie. Now, we're all supposed to be family. He going through something right now. Let him grieve."

"Nall, fuck this nigga. He ain't 'bout that life, Brat. Nigga, since you think you running something, prove that shit. Smoke me, nigga. Right here, in front of everybody. You acting like you ain't afraid to kill shit. Well, I ain't afraid to die. It's either you gon' kill me right here and right now, or you release me from your crew. I ain't feelin' your leadership no more, Blood." I sat my guns on the table and held my arms out like a lowercase T.

Lost Boy closed one eye and aimed at my forehead. "Nigga, I'ma tell you one more time. Sit yo' punk-ass down or I'm smoking you. This yo' last warning. That's on my Blood, nigga."

"Fuck you, Blood. Do what you gotta do," I spat, spit flying out of my mouth and onto his fare.

He frowned and placed his finger around the trigger. "Ah, nigga! You lucky I got respect for your father, 'cause if I didn't, your brains would be splattered all over this floor right now. Take that bitch and that other punk-ass nigga behind you and y'all get the fuck out of my trap. If I catch any of you niggas in my hood ever again, I'm murking you on sight. Ain't no ifs, ands, or buts about it. Bloods, y'all see any of these three, you shoot first and ask questions last. That's an order."

I grabbed my guns off the table and put them on my waist. "I know I ain't the only muthafucka that's tired of being in this crew where the only nigga that matter is Lost Boy. If any of you niggas wanna fuck wit' me, I can guarantee I'll keep you eating real well, where you can take care of your family as well as yourselves. You'll be my equal, but I'll expect you to crush niggas like him: greedy, self-centered, all-about-themself-type niggas that won't even ride for you if somebody in your family get their heads blown off. Fuck type of leader is that?" I shook my head at him.

"Heinous, bounce, nigga. These kats ain't stupid. They know following behind you is a death sentence. I give you two weeks and you'll be in somebody's morgue. Wait 'til Pesos put that bread on your head," he snickered. "Get the fuck out of my shit."

I stepped to the door and held it open. Brat walked out first, followed by Capo. I looked back at Lost Boy and nodded. "Nigga, before it's all said and done, I'ma fuck over both of you niggas since you got the audacity to throw my father's killer in my face. Unlike you, when it's time, I ain't gon' be afraid to pull that trigger. That's my word." I stepped into the hallway and slammed the door.

I knew I was out of my mind. On any other day I would have never disrespected Lost Boy in that fashion, but my mother had broken me. She had always been my best friend and the love of my life.

77

Now that I felt she didn't love me, I was shattered emotionally and spiritually. I didn't give a fuck about death and yearned for somebody to put me out of my misery. On top of that, I was feeling like fuck Lost Boy! I wasn't the type to follow behind no nigga, anyway.

When we got to Brat's red Benz, she waited until I got in the passenger seat and Capo got in the back before she lost her mind. "Nigga! Do you have any idea what the fuck you just did? Huh?" she asked, turning in her seat to look at me.

"Man, fuck them niggas. We gon' start our own crew and get to crushing selfish niggas like him. The three deadliest members of his crew just walked out of those doors, so what the fuck you worried about?" I asked, placing my guns on my lap.

"I'm worried because them niggas don't play fair, and they know where my mama stay. We had a better chance of killing his ass right then and there instead of this cat-and-mouse game. Now we gotta worry about when they gon' try some shit wit' us. Nall, fuck that, Heinous. That was stupid. You know I'll ride with you until the death, but you just got me in some bullshit with our Blood family." She started the ignition and pulled out of the parking spot.

"Aye. Say, Capo?" I turned around to look at him. He had his red rag around his chubby neck. He was brown-skinned with three teardrops under his left eye and a real nappy fro. He was a heavyset dude as well, about my height.

"What's good, bruh?" He curled his lip and

looked over his shoulder out the back window.

"I just wanted to let you know I love you, dawg. And I'ma bust my gun for you until my last breath. You ain't have to do what you did, but I appreciate you just the same. On my word, nigga, I'ma make sure you eat out here in these slums. Just fuck wit' me."

"Man, Brat is my heart, and you're hers. I'm riding with you just as long as she is. Fuck Lost Boy. I ain't never liked that nigga, no way. He ain't 'bout that action like the rest of us."

"Yeah, but still and all, that was suicide. Ain't no way I'm laying my head on the pillow tonight until I can come up with a plan to morgue that nigga. He gotta go. Him and his two Blood guards," Brat said, taking her tech from under her seat and setting it on her lap with a red rag around the handle. "I hope you ready to go to war, Heinous. Both down here in Moe Town and in the Wild Hunnits. We gotta be prepared."

I leaned my seat back and closed my eyes. All I could see was the way my father looked in his casket and the vision of my mother tooting powder off her dresser. I was mentally fucked up and didn't know how I was going to get my mind right enough to be able to formulate a plot to conquer my struggles. I needed an oasis, a way to lean back for a night or something. It was the only way for me to get on point.

Hood Rich

Chapter 7

Instead of Brat going at Lost Boy and his crew that night, I detoured her plans and we wound up at the Diamond Inn Suites. I booked the presidential suite that had a waterfall and a pool. It had two big beds in the room, and they were a short distance from each other. There was a hot tub right next to the patio door that led out to a balcony overlooked downtown Chicago.

My sister's name was Leah. She was 5'2" tall with brown skin and brown eyes. She weighed about 130pounds. All my niggas said she was strapped and bad as hell, but I couldn't really judge her, so I couldn't say.

When I stepped into the presidential suite with Yani under my arm and one of her close girlfriends by the name of Bekah, Leah was sat with her back against the headboard. She had her thighs wide open while Brat held her sex lips apart and ate her pussy for all she was worth. She was moaning so loud at first I thought something was wrong with her. The room smelled like pussy and weed.

Bekah was 5'8" tall and a mix of black and white. She had long, curly hair and a big-ass booty that jiggled every time she took a stem. She really didn't have much in the breast department, maybe a nice B, but her nipples were huge and her breasts were firm. I loved holding them and sucking all over them.

"Now, this what I'm talking about, Heinous. Let's kick this freaky shit off. Your sister over there sounding like they getting it on." She clapped her hands together and kissed me on the cheek, then licked my neck on down to my collar bone.

Yani looked around at her and pushed her back. "Hold on, bitch. You know how this shit go. I kick shit off wit' my nigga first, and you find a way to jump in like double-dutch. Come on, Daddy. Let me get you out of these pants." She grabbed my hand and led me to the same bed Brat and Leah were doing their thing on.

Bekah climbed onto the bed in her short skirt and slid her hand underneath it. She sucked at her bottom lip as Brat ran two fingers in and out of Leah. It didn't bother me, being in the same room while Leah got down, because growing up out mother had been real strict and really didn't let us do nothing. So whenever an opportunity presented itself, me and Leah would sneak our company into our room and get it on. Since my sister went both ways, it helped a lot because she'd often bring home a girl we both could flip. I'd taken more than one virginities on account of my sister. I loved when we fucked hos together, as crazy as that may seem.

Brat picked her face up from between Leah's thighs and wiped her mouth. She smiled at Bekah and pulled down her halter top. "Bitch, take this off, and come over here and join us. I know yo' pussy already wet, ain't it?" She placed her hand underneath Bekah's skirt and rubbed in between her lips before sucking her fingers into her mouth. "Hell yeah."

Bekah pulled her nipples and allowed Brat to

finger her at the same time she fingered Leah. She closed her eyes and moaned, "Ooh, that feel so good." She squeezed her titties together and rocked back and forth on her fingers. "Yes, get all the way in there." She spread her knees on the bed and threw her head back, moaning to the ceiling.

Yani, dropped between my legs and pulled my Gucci jeans down to my ankles and off. Next came my boxers. She took ahold of my pipe and stroked it up and down in her tight fist, looking up at me. "I got you, Daddy. I'ma show these bitches how to suck this dick. Ain't nobody putting mouth on this before I do. You're my daddy."

She licked around the head and sucked it into her mouth, slurping loudly with her cheeks hollowed out. Her mouth felt like a burning furnace. She ran her tongue in circles around my tip, sucking as hard as she could.

My toes curled as I looked to my right and saw Bekah was bent all the way over, her pussy busted open with Brat's fingers running in and out of it at full speed. Seeing that made my dick jump inside of Yani's mouth. I rubbed all over Bekah's ass and slid my finger into her back door. This made her arch her back and look back at me with her tongue in the corner of her mouth.

"Ooh, Heinous. You know you gotta hit that before we leave this hotel. I need you back there."

Brat pulled her down and got to kissing all over her lips. Leah joined the kiss, and the trio started to make out and moan into each other's mouths before

Leah hopped on top of Brat and pulled down Brat's boxers.

Brat already had a strap-on connected around her waist. Leah held it steady while she slowly slid down on it. She closed her eyes and kept her mouth wide open, then slowly her hips got to popping back and forth. The dildo went in and out of her, stretching her wide. "Uh. Uh. Uh. Uh. Damn, Brat. Damn. You so deep," she moaned, riding her like a champion.

Brat rubbed all over her ass and sucked her swinging titties into her mouth, pulling the brown nipples with her teeth and causing Leah to yelp over and over. The more Leah yelped, the faster she rode Brat with her head thrown backward.

Yani stood up and squeezed my hard dick in her hand. She stroked it up and down, then left it up against my belly while she grabbed a handful of Leah's hair and forced her to kiss her lips. They began sucking all over each other. Leah pulled Yani's shirt over her head, then unlatched her bra in the front. Both of Yani's big titties tumbled into the open, the nipples erect and yearning to be sucked. She held them together and allowed Leah to suck them.

Bekah climbed out of the bed, an knelt down in front of me. She took ahold of my dick and licked the opening, kissed all over it, then got to stroking it up and down. "I want you to fuck me so bad with this big-ass dick, Heinous. I love when you stuff me." She opened her thighs wide, fingering herself while she held my dick in her mouth. Her fingers ran in and out of her thick lips. They were slippery. Her fluids dripped out of her and made a puddle on the carpet. "You wanna fuck this mixed pussy?" she asked licking up and down my dick.

I shivered and nodded my head. "Get yo' li'l, thick ass up here. Give me some of that shit." I grabbed her hair roughly and pulled her to her feet.

She stepped in front of me and squatted down so she could run my head in between her sex lips. Her juicy thighs were spread wide. "Aw. Aw. Sss. Aw. I want this dick in me. Fuck this."

She took ahold of the stalk and slowly tried to force me between her lips and into her tight hole, which was giving me a lot of resistance. Her inner lips were scorching hot and leaking. I grabbed her big ass and pulled her to me, kissing all over her lips and sucking on her neck. I cupped both small titties, and loved the feel of them in my hands. Her nipples were out at least an inch or more. The areola was a dark brown, the nipples themselves looked like Tootsie Rolls.

I sucked the right one into my mouth while I cupped her ass. "I want some of this pussy. You ready for me to bust this shit open? You sure you can handle all of this dick? The last time you cried, remember?" I squeezed her ass and slipped my fingers into her box from the back. Bekah was slightly bowlegged, so it was an easy transition. Her fat pussy sucked my fingers into her body as if it was hungry. Once they were inside of her, she got to throwing her ass back on them, so I added a third to get her ready for what I had in mind.

Leah laid Yani back on the bed and opened her pussy lips, licking up and down her slit while she held on to Yani's big titties. I could see Yani's nipples sticking up through the cracks of Leah's fingers.

Yani opened her legs wider and spread her pussy lips for Leah. "Eat me, Leah. Eat this pussy just like yo' brother do every day." She looked over at me and lowered her eyes, smiling.

Brat bent Leah all the way over until her stomach was against Yani's, then she took the strap-on and connected it so it rubbed her clit while she did her thing, took the head of the black monster, and slammed it into Leah with no mercy.

"Aw, fuck! Fuck, Brat! There you go, bitch! There you go!" She kissed Yani's lips and slammed back into Brat. Her ass jiggled.

Brat smacked her across it and rubbed all over the caramel moon. I could see the dildo going in and out of her pussy, the lips sucking at it, trying to keep it inside before Brat slammed it back deep into her belly. She'd smack her ass after every three pumps.

Bekah pushed me back on the bed and straddled my waist. She placed one thick thigh on each side of my waist, found my dick, and slid down the knob with her eyes rolling into the back of her head. "Oh shit. Oh shit. Oh shit. Okay, okay, it's in me now. It's in me." She took a deep breath and exhaled loudly.

I grabbed her waist and sat up. "Ride this dick, bitch. You up here now." I bear hugged her waist and bounced her up and down, making sure she was taking my whole pipe. Her insides were as hot as an oven on broil.

She wrapped her arms around my neck, and placed her cheek against mine, shivering like crazy. "Aw. Aw. Aw. Aw. Aw. Aw. Um. Yes. Yes. Yes. Fuck. Me. Heinous. Aw. Shit. It's. So big. It hurts." She bounced up and down. Her soft ass would land in my lap before it rose again. The nipples on her breasts poked at my collarbone. She smelled like Cashmere Gold. Her body was warm and soft.

I looked past her shoulder as she rode me like a champion and saw Brat fucking Leah so hard the dildo fell out of her, leaking with her juices. It landed on the bed with a thump before Leah reached under herself and slid it back into her gaping hole. She slammed back into Brat and fingered Yani with three digits. Her entire wrist was dripping from Yani's pussy juices. Yani held her thighs wide open and squeezed her titties together.

"I'm coming. I'm coming, Heinous! Oh my God, this dick so big. It's. So. Big," she hollered and got to fucking me as hard and fast as she could before shaking like crazy. She bit into my neck, and screamed in my ear so loud it started to ring.

My dick slid in and out of her hole. I gripped her ass and made her keep going even though I could feel her cum saturating my balls and wetting my thighs. I felt like I was ready to cum in her. The scent of pussy was heavy in the room. It smelt good to me. Intoxicating. I wished I could have breathed that air every day, all day.

Bekah stood up and released my long, glistening dick from her pussy. It looked like a slippery baseball bat with veins running through it. She bent over the bed and spread her thighs, reached under her belly, and opened her lips for me. "Hit this pussy from the back. Hit it like you did last time," she groaned. Even though she was acting tough, she looked scared as hell with her bottom lip quivering and her arms shaking. A clear string of gel hung from her left pussy lip, all the way down to the carpet of the hotel. All around her brown, wrinkled lips were juices she's secreted. It looked hot. Her pussy was fat and a little swollen. I just had to hit that some more.

Before I could slide back into her, Yani hopped out of the bed and knelt before me, sucking my dick into her mouth. At tasting Bekah's cum, she closed her eyes and really went to town on my pole, rubbing in between Bekah's thighs.

"I'm coming, Brat. I'm coming!" Leah hollered. She fell to the bed with her face against the sheets, her eyes closed tightly as she shook over and over again.

Brat pulled her huge dildo out of her and ran it all around Leah's asshole. "You gon' let me fuck this ass, Leah? Huh? Just let me hit this it this one time. I'll change your life." She rubbed all over Leah's ass.

Leah shook her head. "Nall, I ain't ready for that yet. I already told you that. Maybe another time." She got to her knees and slid off the bed. She knelt beside Yani and rubbed all over her titties with a hand between her legs. "Yani, I want some more of this pussy, baby. You gon' rub this up against mine some more?" she asked, sucking Yani's neck.

Yani stood up and bent over. "Girl, I need some of his dick. Come on and fuck me, Heinous. Fuck me way harder than you just did Bekah. She can't handle your shit like I can."

"This ain't no competition, Yani. I just like fucking Heinous because he know how to."

Brat stepped behind her and forced her face into the bed. "Shut up, bitch, and give me this pussy." She lined herself up and shoved into her from the back so hard Bekah shrieked.

"Wait! Wait! Wait! What. Are. You. Doing? Oh. Shit," she moaned while Brat went to town on her ass like a savage.

I already knew what this was about. Anytime me and Brat fucked hos together, we always wound up competing. She didn't like when females gave me my props and didn't acknowledge she knew how to get down, too, so she'd often make a mockery of the bitch she was fucking just to prove a point. But I was always up for the challenge. I honestly didn't think she could fuck with my dick game. Not only was my shit almost eleven inches and thick as a wrist, but I knew how to fuck because I loved pussy just as much as she did, if not more.

I picked Yani up and slammed her onto the bed, laid her on her side, and forced her thick thigh to her shoulder before I slid in and got to killing her pussy while Leah held her sex lips apart for me. My dick was like a battering ram.

"Get it, Daddy. Get it. Fuck yo' baby. Fuck me. Aw. Aw. Oh. Oh. Yes. Yes. Harder, Daddy. Harder," she whimpered.

Leah grabbed ahold of her right breast and slid a finger up her own pussy, fucking it in and out. "Kill her pussy, Heinous. I love when you be fucking these hos." She placed her mouth over Yani's and they began to make out.

Brat was fucking Bekah so hard she was crying. Her face was balled up. The constant sounds of their skin slapping together coupled with that of mine and Yani's sounded like somebody was in the room being smacked on the back over and over again. The bed rocked back and forth, beating against the wall.

I continued to pipe Yani down. Her pussy was so good. Nice, dripping wet, and hot. It felt like a marshmallow inside of her. Her walls were trembling from the assault.

Leah pinched Yani's clit and ran her thumb in a circle around it while my dick shot in and out of her. She continued to finger herself, and every now and then she would lean down so they could kiss. Yani reached between Leah's thighs and replaced Leah's fingers with her own. The next thing I knew, Leah was lying on her side, eating Yani's pussy from the back while I fucked her as hard as I could.

That sight became too much for me. I couldn't take it no more. The scent of pussy, the sight of Brat fucking the shit out of Bekah, then Leah eating Yani's pussy from the back while my dick sawed in and out of her, busting her wide open. It was all too much. I felt my excitement building inside of me. My balls tingled, and then my penis head got so sensitive it made Yani's hot marshmallow feel like a slice of heaven. I couldn't take it no more. I tensed up, and the next thing I knew, I was coming deep in Yani's pussy in strong spasms.

I pulled it out and busted all over her thick thighs. My cream shot out of me and started to land all over her and Leah before she jumped back and wiped it off of her face. I couldn't help it. Yani's pussy was that good.

Bekah slammed back into Brat five quick times and screamed at the top of her lungs. I wanted to smack the shit out of her because she was so loud. And because she had been, I knew Brat was gon' make it seem like she had won because she'd made her bitch scream the loudest, but I wasn't trying to hear that shit. I knew she couldn't fuck wit' my bidness.

***

A few hours later we wound up in the big pool with Cardi B's *Bickenhead* banging through the speakers. Yani sat with her ass in my lap. Leah was in front of her, and they were making out like horny teenagers. Bekah was in front of Brat with her titties in her hand.

Brat sucked all over her neck before leaning over toward me. "I just got a text from that fool, School

Boy. He trying to fuck wit' us. Say he wanna meet up in the morning to discuss some of the shit you talking about before you left out of the meeting the other day." She kissed Bekah on the back of the neck and slid her hand down her stomach onto her bald pussy underneath the water. The pool was so clear I could see everything.

"Ain't that fool School Boy been running under him longer than we have?" I asked, feeling Leah reach between Yani's thighs. My dick was in the right crease of Yani's leg. I guessed Leah was trying to find her opening, so she nudged my dick out of the way wit' her knuckle before she slid two fingers into Yani. Yani arched her back and continued to tongue her down.

"Yeah, he have, but it ain't no secret Lost Boy been fucking School Boy's baby mother for the last three months. He already caught them twice. The whole hood been talking about it. I figured if anybody would cross over and fuck wit' us, it would be him. He probably want that bitch-nigga Lost Boy off the face of the earth just as much as you do."

Yani was slowly riding Leah's fingers. Her ass would pop back into my lap, and her cheeks would smash against me, then bounce forward. I could hear her moaning, and it was turning me on. I was trying to stay focused on what Brat was talking about, but my dick had a mind of its own.

"You don't think this nigga on no bullshit or nothin'?" I slid my hand into Yani's ass crack and slipped a finger into her back door. My dick was still laid up against the right corner of her pussy lips. Leah was fingering her so fast her arm was splashing in the water. She was whimpering and biting into her lip.

"I think if that nigga Lost Boy was on any bullshit wit' you, you would have never been able to walk out of there the other day. He would have killed all of us, and we would have took a bunch of them, too. It ain't sweet. But nall, I say we hear him out and see what it do from there. If he on some bullshit, we're killas. We'll know it."

I felt my dick being squeezed under the water, and then it was lined up to go into Yani's cat again. "A'ight, we'll fuck wit' that nigga first thing in the morning. First, I gotta get me some more of this pussy."

Brat scrunched her face and tried to look at what was going on underwater. "Dang, what y'all got going on over there?"

Leah rubbed along Yani's back as I bent her over. "Don't worry about it. You focus in on that red bitch in front of you."

She rolled her eyes and took her bra back off.

Hood Rich

Chapter 8

The next morning we met up with School Boy at his crib on 54th and Aberdeen. As we were pulling up, his baby mother was hollering out the window of her car, holding up her middle finger. "Fuck you, School Boy. You need to get yo' shit together with yo' insecure ass. Don't worry about if I'm doing me. Nigga, you just do you!" she snapped before storming away from the curb, leaving tire marks in the street.

I stepped up on his porch and looked over my shoulder. The block was packed already. There were people sitting on their porches two- and three-deep. Kids were running up and down the sidewalk, chasing one another. Little girls were jumping rope and singing ghetto nursery rhymes while they did their thing. It was about ninety degrees outside, hot and extremely humid. My head was already pounding because of the bright sunlight.

School Boy waved us inside after looking both ways down each side of the block. "Y'all come on in. We got a lot of shit to discuss," he grumbled. He sounded choked up. One of them sucka-for-love-type niggas, I was guessing. He was dressed in black basketball shorts and a beater over a bulletproof vest.

"Say, nigga, I'm letting you know before we even step into this bitch that if anything look fishy, I ain't aiming fo' yo' vest, my nigga. I'ma pop that head like a big-ass zit. That's on my mother." I slid my hand under my shirt to emphasize my point.

He shrugged his shoulders. "To be honest with you, Heinous, I wouldn't even give a fuck right now. My bitch got me all fucked up, her and that cut-throat-ass Lost Boy. Now come in, nigga."

He held the door open and I stepped into his small apartment that smelled like cigarettes. I hated that smell. That shit had my head pounding worse than it had been before. I felt like I was ready to puke. "Nigga, it stank in here. You ain't got no incense or nothing?" I pinched my nose and scrunched my face. I was seconds away from telling him we was gon' hold our meeting in the back yard where there was fresh air. I didn't care if it was hot outside. At least out there I could breathe without wanting to throw up.

He kicked a Tickle-Me-Elmo doll out of the way that was laying in the middle of the floor with roaches crawling all over it. "Yeah, I got some Somali Rose ones I bought from the old head on the expressway exit. I'ma light one of them real quick. I got you." He walked toward the back of the house, and left me and Brat in the front room where there was a three-piece furniture set that looked like it'd seen better days. The couches were white leather, but the leather was scuffed and worn. There was a big screen television against the wall and a stereo system that had to be from the early nineties.

"Bruh, grab a few of them bitches," I hollered, and was debating on whether I should sit on his furniture or not. There were cockroaches crawling all over the walls and the floor. I felt so uncomfortable being there.

"Say, Heinous, I can already tell you ain't feeling his spot, but hold fast, nigga. Don't get to ribbing him and making him feel some type of way. Let's see what he's getting at first. Do you hear me?" she asked, looking serious.

I stepped on a big-ass roach that had an egg hanging out of its ass. It popped under my shoe. I looked toward the couch and saw about fifteen more crawling from under it. I was disgusted.

"Did you hear what I said to you?" Brat asked, growing irritated.

"Yeah, I got you. Just chill. Even though you gotta admit homie nasty as hell. I'd whoop my bitch ass if I lived with her and she allowed for the crib to get this popped. Fuck that."

Brat jerked her head backward. "Nigga, it ain't no bitch's job to clean the house by herself. If you want it clean, you better hop yo' lanky-ass up and handle that bitness." She smacked her lips. "You think just because you a pretty boy and shit that a bitch supposed to do everything for you? Nigga, please." She rolled her eyes. She was dressed in a black and red Gucci fit. Her hair was in single braids, and she had black and red barrettes on the end of them. Her swag was on a hunnit. I had to give her props on that.

"Fuck you," I laughed.

School Boy walked into the room with three incense sticks lit. He stuck them into a few mini-holes in the wall, then plopped on the sofa. As soon

97

as he did, a bunch of roaches started to scatter all over the place. It was crazy.

"Why y'all still standin' up? Have a seat." He nodded at the couch across from him.

As much as I didn't want to, I sat beside Brat and tried to focus on the task at hand. "A'ight, we sitting. Now, what's good?"

He took a deep breath and exhaled. "In order for you to do your own thing, you're going to have to kill Lost Boy. The way that nigga was talking when you left was crazy. You're living on a short clock, according to him." He pulled a pack of Newports from the crack of the couch and got ready to light it.

I held up my hand. "Please don't, bruh. Look, we can blow some of this Kush. Them squares stank like a muthafucka." I pulled a Garcia Vega from my inside pocket and licked all around it. "G'on, finish what you were saying. Make sure you tell us why all of the sudden you trying to get down with us, too. This seem a li'l fishy to me."

Brat scooted to the edge of the couch and looked him over real suspicious-like. Her hand slipped under her Gucci top.

School Boy slid the cigarettes back into the crease of the couch. "Anyway, like I was saying, that fool want you two dead. But not only him. So does Pesos and a few other niggas that's calling shots throughout the city. It turns out when y'all shot up Golden Gate Park, Pesos was holding a get-together to squash a bunch of beef with a few other crews he'd been beefing with over the last year. Now, I know you couldn't have known that, but it just so happens y'all's bullets hit and killed three different dudes from three separate organizations. Now their bosses are calling for your head, Heinous. The only reason Lost Boy ain't kill you a few days ago is because he was given the order to leave you alive because Pesos want to personally cut your head off and hand it over to Lloyd, the chief of the Gangsta Crips out in the Hunnits. He's been giving Pesos the most problems. If Pesos doesn't deliver your head to him within the next few weeks, it's going to be an all-out war. So, it's either you're going to flee from the city with your life and let whatever Pesos did to you and your father slide, or you're going to go at him full-force to avenge your Pops. If you go that route, he won't be the only major player in the game you'll have to worry about. Shit could get dangerous."

I scoffed and nodded my head. "Oh yeah. So it take all of them niggas to link up to come at li'l ol' me, huh? Well, ain't that somethin'."

"It ain't just you, Heinous. I'm riding with you, through and through. Dem niggas come at you, they gotta come at me, too. That's all I'm saying." Brat, stood up and began to pace the floor. "So, if you know all of this, why you call me over here right now, making it seem like you're ready to switch sides and fuck wit' us? It don't sound like that would be a smart move."

"Pay me to be your inside man. I've rolled beside Lost Boy for over ten years. I know everybody in the city that he know. If these dudes coming together so they can take you out of the game, you need to get them before they get you. I got the 411 on everybody. I'm talking where they lay their heads on down to who babysit their kids on a daily basis. All I need you to do is hit my hand and let me keep on doing my thing inside of the Blood Stones for the next few weeks so I can strengthen my connections. Once that happens, I'll let you know. Then I want the ultimate payoff."

I handed him the blunt and watched him take five quick pulls and inhale all of the smoke. "And what is this ultimate payoff?" I asked, looking over at Brat. She stopped mid-pace and beamed her eyes on him.

"I want you to kill Lost Boy and my baby mother, Annya." He sat back on the couch, and frowned.

That caught me off guard. "How many shorties you got by Annya, man?" I really didn't give a fuck about whacking Lost Boy and his bitch, but it just seemed like an odd request. How many niggas wanted to see the mother of their children murdered? That was cold-blooded and low-down. I knew I was going to have to watch this nigga very, very closely.

He shrugged his shoulders. "It don't matter. I'm gon' give you the low-down on every major nigga who want you lying in a coffin, and you'll do your thing. After I handle the business I need to, then you'll knock my B.M. and Lost Boy off. Either take the deal or don't, although I think it sounds like one hell of a trade-off to me. I'll even make it more sweeter if you'll fuck wit' me on this. I'll give you the low-down on all of Lost Boy's plugs. You can knock their asses off and really come up. But I'd have to have half of all of the licks you hit. I got plans on becoming the next king of the Blood Stones. I'll need some form of capitol in order to do that."

I was trying to see what was lying beneath the surface with this nigga. I knew he couldn't be as thorough as he was making himself out to be to us. If he was willing to have the mother of his children murdered along with the man he's been under for more than a decade, then what amount of loyalty could he really have inside of him? I wasn't seeing none, nor did I trust him.

I made up my mind right then that before it was all said and done, I was going to kill School Boy. It would be the only thing that made sense. Of course I would use him to knock off the other enemies, but in my book he was one as well. When it came to the game, a nigga with no loyalty was the worst kind of monster in the field. He had no attachments. I was wondering how he felt about his kids if he could so easily kill their mother. I needed to find at least one attachment or weakness I could use against him down the line as either a bargaining tool or something I could develop a strategy from.

"Bruh, you sure your li'l ones gon' be good if we hit their mother? I mean, you definitely got a deal, and I'ma handle that bidness anyway, but I just want you to think about that for a second. What would you tell them?"

He looked at me for a long time with his upper lip curled. "I don't give a fuck about them li'l bitches.

They gon' grow up to be hos, just like their mother. Fuck them. Fuck what they think," he spat and jumped up. "Look, we got a deal or not?"

I had my hand gripped tightly around the handle of my .40 Glock. "Yeah, nigga, we do. You hold up your end, and I'll hold up mine. Hit me up when you get the first bit of information that will be useful to me."

He wiped sweat from his big, bald head. "I already got it. The nigga's name is Tommy Kid. He's Lloyd's right-hand man, and this weekend he gon' be laid up with his sixteen-year-old cousin out in Milwaukee. They got the Summer Fest going on up there, but he's staying at Lloyd's sister's crib while they're out of town on Eighty-Eighth and Greenfield Street. It's a white and brown house, three down from the alley. You get out there before Friday and knock him off, that will cripple Lloyd. He's beefing with some Kings up there. The last I heard, they were supposed to be on a peace treaty, but if his right-hand man wind up dead, all of his army's fighting power will be projected at them instead of you. Then you can creep in through his back door and murder his ass. I'm giving you his info first because he the one that's gon' come at your head when he get back in town, according to Lost Boy."

I nodded. "A'ight, let me get that. I appreciate this, my nigga. Let's keep shit on the up-and-up so we can both reach the destinations we're shooting for."

He reached out his hand and I shook it. "Let's

fuck these niggas over. Blood in, my nigga."

***

My mother answered the door sometime later that afternoon with her hair all over the place and bags under her eyes. She was wearing a sheer white bra that looked dingy over the same color and poorly-conditioned panties. After she let me in, she walked away, scratching her head and mumbling to herself.

I looked around her pad with a scowl on my face. It looked like it had not been cleaned in at least two weeks, and it smelled like funk. I locked the door and covered my mouth with my right hand in pure shock. For as long as I'd known my mother, she'd always been the cleanest person I'd known, outside of myself.

I stepped into the dining room. The entire house was dark and had the shades drawn She was sitting at the dining room table in front of a baking sheet with a pile of heroin on top of it. She had four evenly-spaced lines in front of her and a straw in her right hand. She tooted a line loudly and pinched her nose. Seconds later she tooted a line up her other nostril and started coughing. The sound of Mary J. Blige's *My Life* played out of her speakers.

She ran her fingers through her hair and looked up at me. "I can't stop doing this stuff, son. My whole life I watched my mother and father go crazy over this poison, and I've always said I would never mess with it, but now I can't stop. I need it every second of every day. Even when I'm asleep, I'm dreaming about it. But you know what? I don't hurt over your father the way I used to." She leaned forward in the chair and closed her eyes. I could hear her snoring.

I stood watching her for thirty seconds, and then she snapped out of it. "Yeah, Mama ain't hurting the way she was before I discovered this."

I knelt in front of her and placed my hands on her knees. "Mama, you're killing yourself right now. You're better than this. When was the last time you were at church?" I asked, feeling a lump form in my throat.

She dozed back off with her head cocked to the right. She snored through her nose, then ran her hand over her face. "Church? I ain't been to church since your father's funeral. I can't go through them doors feeling like I'm feeling. I would only imagine his casket is somewhere in the building. I ain't ready, son. I feel safe right here. I talk to Jesus all day long. He hears. Oh, you better believe he hears." She scratched her arm until it started to bleed. I expected her to wipe the blood away, but instead she picked up the straw and got ready to toot another line.

I slapped all of her materials onto the floor, along with the heroin. "I'm not about to let you do this to yourself. You're better than this." I was fuming. My mother had always been the strongest woman I'd ever known. To see her in such a state made me feel weak and incapable of handling my tasks in front of me. My mother had always been my source of strength, and to see her conquered by a form of the devil was almost enough to bring me to my knees.

She dropped down and stuck her face in the carpet, trying to snort the dope from it. "What's your problem, Jahrome? Do you know how much that cost me?" she screamed, rubbing her face in the pile of work.

I snatched her up and carried her to the back room, slamming the door. "Mama, I'm finna get you some help. You ain't about to go out like this."

I rushed into the bathroom and turned on the tub, making sure it was nothing but warm water running out of the faucet. Then I ran back into the room where I'd left her. The door was wide open. I found my mother in the dining room, shoving pinches of dope up her nose. She sniffed as hard as she could, choking on it. "Ack! Ack! It's mine. It's mine."

I picked her back up and carried her into the bathroom with her legs kicking wildly. She twisted in my arms and screamed, "Let me go! Let me go, Jahrome! Get your freaking hands off of me! You're not my damn father! I'm your mother!"

I carried her over to the tub and dropped her inside of it. The water splashed and spilled over the top. She acted like a cat instead of a human being. Her eyes bucked. She took in a big gasp of air and struggled to use the rim of the tub to get out of it. "I'ma kill you. I'ma kill you, Jahrome. I swear!" she screamed.

Tears slid down my face. I couldn't believe I had to do what I was doing. I ripped her bra away from her body, took the loofa from the corner of the tub, and dipped it into the water. "Stop fighting me, Mama. I gotta get you clean, 'cause you going into rehab tonight," I swore. My tears dripped off my chin. My heart was splitting in two. I'd never in a million years imagined I would have gotten to this point.

I held my forearm against her chest, forcing her against the side of the tub while I squirted body wash into the loofa. She scratched at my arms. "You're gon' blow my high, Jahrome. Please stop, son. You're going to blow my high," she cried, laying back and giving up her fight.

I dunked the loofa into the water and grabbed her right arm, washing under it. "I'm not gon' lose you to this dope, Mama. I need you, and so does Leah. We're still here. You can't forget about us. It ain't fair." My nose was running, and I couldn't stop the tears falling from my eyes. I wanted my queen back. I was wishing she had never tried to destroy the heroin in the first place, because had she not, we wound've never been here. Then again, it all came back to Pesos' punk-ass, because had he never did what he did, my father would still be alive and my mother would have never discovered the heroin to begin with. Everything that had gone wrong came back to him in some way or another. I couldn't wait to end his life. I wanted it so bad I could envision it.

My mother broke into a fit of tears. She took off her panties, dropped them on the floor beside the tub, and laid back. "Help me, son. I need your help. I need that dope so bad, and if you leave me alone with it,

I'm going to do it." She shook her head and began to bawl her eyes out.

I swallowed the lump in my throat and continued to wash her. I'd never felt weaker than I did taking care of her. I'd never seen my mother lower than she was. Growing up, I had always looked to her for strength more than I did my own father. My mother was a faithful woman. She had principles and took her faith seriously. She stood firm on two feet even though her childhood had been the worst, raised by two parents who barely made sure she ate at night. Both suffered from the illness of drug and alcohol addiction. Against all odds, she was able to make it out alive, graduating both high school and college to obtain her Master's Degree in Theology. I looked up to her. Whenever I felt weak, I simply remembered how strong my queen was and reminded myself I'd come from her. She was my everything.

I stood her up and washed every nook and cranny of her body before she sat back down and I started on her hair. Once that was all lathered with shampoo, I let the plug out of the drain and turned on the shower for her, ready to close the curtain.

She grabbed my neck and kissed my cheek. "I'm so sorry, baby. I'll get better. I promise, I'll get better. I'm just lost right now." She lowered her head as the water beat down on her back, popping off of it and onto the floor mat.

"Mama, the Word says you are supposed to first seek the Kingdom of God, and everything else will be handed to you. Start there, and I'll do my part. I'm not giving up on you. You're the strongest person in this world. I look up to you."

She nodded her head and wiped snot from her upper lip. "Okay, baby. Okay, you're so, so right. I'll check in to rehab tonight."

Chapter 9

It was three days later, and I couldn't get my mother off my mind. As promised, she'd allowed me to check her into rehab after she finished showering. I helped her get dressed, and off we went.

Before she entered the facility, she promised me she was going to give it her all. She told me to pray for her and speak into existence her getting better, so I walked around for the next few days doing exactly that. I was even praying for her under my breath as the Li'l Wayne and Jadakiss *Gotti* album was banging through the speakers of my black and gray Lexus. I was sitting in the passenger seat while Brat drove, a Tech in her lap sitting on top of a red rag.

She turned down the music when we pulled up a block from where Lloyd's right-hand man was supposed to be shacked up with his little cousin. She looked over at me with a frown. "Jo, what's good wit' you? You ain't said shit since we left the Windy. If you having second thoughts, you better let me know right now." She hit the power button, shutting the system off.

"Nah, we already here. I was just thinking about my mother. You know I had to put her in rehab a few days ago. I'm just hoping she's okay. I miss her like a muthafucka."

"That's why we gotta start busting these niggas' heads and getting they ass out of the way. Keeping it real, her being in rehab is the safest place for her right now while this war is going on. I'd hate to see one of them niggas target her or Leah over some shit we been in the streets doing. But you know how Chicago is. Everybody dirty in that muthafucka." She tucked the Tech in her bag and grabbed two hand pistols from under her seat. "Let's kill some shit, nigga. Take one of these silencers, too." She pulled one out of her bra, exposing her big, brown nipple to me accidentally.

"Yeah, let's make this shit happen. No mercy, either."

***

Brat stood on the side of the two-story house while I walked up to the door and rang the doorbell. It was about 9 o'clock p.m. There were a bunch of lightning bugs flying through the air, along with mosquitoes. I was standing there on the porch getting ate up. By the time somebody came on the other side of the door, I was irritated and ready to kill up some shit.

The curtain on the door was moved to the side, and I was met by a gorgeous teen who looked to be about sixteen or seventeen. "Can I help you?" she asked with a curious look on her face. She looked as if she was a mix of black and Hispanic. Her face was bronze, and she had shoulder-length, curly hair.

"Yeah, your uncle Lloyd told me to come holler at Tommy Kid. He here, ain't he?" I asked with a smile on my face. I was hoping she was one of those sheltered, naive little girls.

My heart damn near skipped a beat when I heard her unlocking the door. "Oh yeah, he's here. He's in the back taking a shower." She opened the door and stepped to the side, waving me through.

My heart was pounding in my chest. The first thing I smelled was perfume and a strong odor of sex. She was dressed in daisy dukes that were all up in her crease over a halter top that stopped just below the swells of her breasts. I could tell she wasn't wearing a bra because I could see the bottoms of her yellow titties perfectly.

I upped my .40, pressed it to her forehead, and grabbed her around the throat. "Check this out, shorty. Don't give me a reason to kill you. I come for Tommy Kid's life, not yours. Now, I need you to tell me how many more people are here."

Brat slipped into the house behind me and closed the door. Her red rag was pulled all the way over her face, leaving only enough room for her to see. "What's the deal? Ice that li'l bitch," she demanded before creeping into the house, leaning forward.

"I got this. Dude should be in the bathroom taking a shower. Is he the only one here, shorty?"

She nodded her head as tears sailed down her cheeks and over my wrist. My hand remained around her throat.

"Where is the bathroom?" I loosened my hand just enough for her to talk.

"It's all the way in the back of the house and to the right. You have to go through the kitchen. Please don't take my life. I'm just a kid."

I stepped behind her and wrapped my arm around her neck. "Just shut up and let's go." I forced her to take step after step while Brat stayed low and made her way to the back of the house. I had my gun raised, on point just in case something jumped out at us.

By the time we made it into the kitchen. Lloyd's little cousin was in full-on tears. "Bitch, shut up and lay right there." I flung her li'l pretty-ass to the floor and stepped my foot on her back. I then signaled Brat to open the bathroom door with my gun. I knelt down with my knee in Lloyd's cousin's back. "Go."

Brat tried the knob and it turned. She twisted it all the way and slowly pulled the door open. I raised my gun, ready to blast.

As soon as the door opened all the way, I was able to make out Tommy Kid sitting on the toilet with a cigarette in his mouth and his boxers around his ankles. He had his eyes closed, nodding his head up and down to the Li'l Uzi Vert coming out of the radio in the bathroom.

I jumped up as fast as I could and rushed his ass, slamming the gun against the side of his head so hard he flew off the toilet after skeeting blood across the wall.

"Aw, man! What the fuck is this?" he hollered, trying to get up. There was a big gash in his head that was leaking like a holey pitcher of red Kool-Aid.

I grabbed him by the throat and slammed the gun into his face over and over, bashing his shit in. "Bitch. Nigga. You. Supposed. To. Be. Killing. Me?" I growled, whipping him back-to-back.

"Stop it! You're killing him!" Lloyd's niece yelled. She jumped from the floor to come and help. "Stop it!"

Brat snatched her up and slammed her to the floor with so much force it caused the refrigerator door to open. "You li'l bitch. Aw, you wanna help somebody?" She wrapped two hands around her neck and started to squeeze as hard as she could, choking the dear life out of her while she kicked her legs, exposing the fact she wasn't wearing panties under her daisy dukes.

I slammed Tommy Kid's face into the wall, then dunked his head into the toilet full of shit he'd left behind. I could hear him gurgling on the shitty water. "You bitch-nigga, you can't kill me. You don't even know who you're fucking with, do you?" I pulled his head out of the toilet and flung him to the floor, stepping back with my gun pointed at him. "Why do your boss want me dead?"

He struggled to catch his breath. His face had turned a bright shade of red. There was shit smashed against his forehead and cheek. It was that runny, green stuff, too. It smelled horrible.

He held his hands in front of his face. "Who are you, cuz? I don't even know who the fuck you is," he struggled to breathe. Blood ran out of the wounds on his face and forehead. One of his teeth was missing. I didn't know if I did it or it had already been that way.

"Heinous, muthafucka! That's who I am. Now, why do yo' boss want me dead?"

113

Brat slammed her fist into the girl's face over and over again. I saw she was already knocked out cold. The kitchen floor was a bloody mess, yet Brat continued to serve the girl up on a vicious platter. Her fist beat against her facial structure, then she grabbed her by the sides of her face and started to bang the back of her head into the kitchen floor.

"You killed his son, man. His son was out there balling at the park that day you shot it up. He caught two to the neck. He was visiting from Baltimore. The streets say your gun killed him. That's why he want you dead. But the burden is supposed to be on Pesos, not me. I ain't got shit to do with it." He scooted backward and tried to sit up.

"You're his right-hand man though, ain't you?" I asked, clenching my jaw.

"Yeah, but that don't mean I got shit to do with what he got going on. I'm a hustler, my nigga. I got hittas to handle my bidness for me. That's below my pay grade." He put his fingers to his lip and saw it was leaking blood. He shook his head. "This fucked up. What I gotta do to get out of this jam?"

Brat put her pistol to the little girl's forehead and pulled the trigger. The gun jumped in her hand and a big spark came out of it with the sound of a dull firecracker. The girl's head jerked on her neck before a puddle of blood formed around her from the neck on up.

"Ain't shit you can do to get out of this one, homeboy. You niggas want it wit' me? A'ight, let's get it, then. You're second down."

"Nall, man. Aye, look, I can help you knock Lloyd off. Plus I got the combinations to all of his safes. I can tell you where they are and how much is in each one. Trust me, Jo, I'm worth more to you alive than dead. Shid, fuck that nigga."

I couldn't believe how disloyal Chicago niggas were these days. Muthafuckas was so quick to give up their right-hand mans instead of dying with honor. That shit baffled me. I didn't give a fuck how much money was involved, I was killing this fuck-nigga in cold blood. It's like the pussy in him just irked my soul.

Brat stood beside me with her chest heaving up and down like she was out of breath. She tried to move me out of the way so she could get at Tommy Kid, but I stopped her.

"Nall, I got this." I turned back to him. "Yeah, all that fuck-shit sound real good. But nigga, if yo' right-hand mans can't even trust you, what make you think, I will?" I hopped forward and raised my foot in the air before bringing it down as hard as I could right in the middle of his chest. I could feel his rib cage snap under the weight of my foot.

He wound up slammed against the side of the tub. He stood up with his chest sunken in, gasping for air. I could see his rib bones were sticking through the skin in his midsection. "Uh! Uh!" He reached out for me and fell to his knees, struggling to breathe. His eyes tried to roll into the back of his head.

I smacked him across the face with my pistol and waited for him to fall on his back before I pressed the barrel of my heater to his forehead and pulled the trigger, sending him to the Reaper.

I stood looking down on him for a few seconds, with my top lip curled. I knew he was going to be the first of many. Whenever there was a hit placed on a nigga's name in the city of Chicago, it was only a matter of time before someone picked up the bounty and tried to kill the nigga every chance they got. I didn't know how many predators were on my heels already. All I could do was take out the major players and hope I would still be standing at the end of the game.

***

For a majority of the ride back to Chicago, me and Brat barely uttered a word to each other. We sat back, listening to Biggie's *What's Beef* on repeat. I had so many things going through my head that I was catching a migraine. Nothing to me was more important than the safety and wellbeing of first my mother, then my sister and Yani. I knew I was entering a war with a bunch of savages who got down like I did. Even if they didn't personally pick up the strap, they had hittas who would never hesitate. Whenever a nigga was able to sit back and call shots, it made things a lot easier because they weren't risking their own life. They were risking the lives of the men who ran under them. The more pawns a nigga had in a game, the more moves they were able to make without losing valuable pieces.

In my case, I was the most valuable piece, followed by Brat, then Capo. I looked as Brat as my queen because I knew she would make moves all kinds of ways to fuck a nigga over. She'd stand beside me and protect me at all costs, do whatever it would take to make sure I was never cornered and mated. She was my most valuable piece after myself.

Capo, on the other hand, was like my bishop. He moved in the lanes he was familiar with in the slums. He'd mastered those lanes, and if ever a muthafucka got caught slipping fucking wit' the homie in those lanes, they'd get their ass busted. He was very important to me, as well, because I needed him to pull us a bunch of head-busters from those lanes so we could build up an army that would go at the necks of the opposition. An army of pawns, low-level niggas who were expendable. Soldiers neither of us really cared about, but ones who were needed to go at the enemy. The more pawns I had, the better chance I had at withstanding and slaying my opponents. Even those we were the strongest pieces on the board, the man with the most pawns and power pieces in the end always won.

Brat turned down the Biggie track and smiled at me, nodding her head in a 'what up?' motion. "Nigga, your lips moving but, I ain't heard shit you said. What's good?" she asked, switching lanes.

"Aw, shit. I was just over here going through some stuff in my head. If that nigga was telling the truth, then we gotta get us some soldiers to go at these niggas. Ain't no telling what direction that fool Pesos

117

gon' try and come from, so we gotta be ready at every turn. Not only that, we gotta go at him before he come at us. You already know how the game go. I'm ready to start killing up some shit. It's the only way we gon' make it out of this war that's brewing." I pushed in the car lighter and took my blunt out of the ashtray. I was fien'ing for that heroin, and I was trying not to think about it even though my body was aching.

"Shid, we gotta put up some chips, then. If we can come up with, like, a hundred bands real quick, then we can get us some li'l grimy niggas that's bout' that action. But in order for them to ride for us, they gotta have some chips in their pockets. It's the law of the land. Niggas ride for whoever's putting food on their table and clothes on their backs. It's been like that ever since all of the real heads of these organizations out here got either killed or indicted."

I nodded. I was counting the money in my safe inside of my head. I knew for a fact I had over a hundred bands put up. I was thinking, like, a hundred fifteen, but I wasn't sure. Either way, I knew I had at least that. If that was all it was going to take in order for me to begin building my army, then I had to drop that paper. "I think I got something like that put up. See what you can pull together, and in the meantime I'ma see what's good with that nigga School Boy. He might have some licks for us and be able to tell us where the enemy is coming from next. So far he one-for-one. We gotta watch this nigga closely too, though. In my mind, he got an expiration date just like Lost Boy do."

Brat nodded. "If it was up to me, we'd stank both of they ass on the same night and be done wit' it. I don't trust that nigga as far as I can throw him."

"You the only one I trust, queen. Fuck the world if it ain't about you and our bond. I bleed for you, my nigga. Word up," I said, shaking up with her.

"You're blood of my blood. I go 'til the death of me, bruh. That is on my mother." She turned the Biggie *What's Beef* track back on. "These niggas don't know who they fucking wit', Heinous. But they gon' learn real fast, though. Real fast, Blood!" She slammed her hands on the steering wheel and sat back.

"It's kill season, Brat. On everything I love."

Hood Rich

Chapter 10

My mother stayed in rehab for two weeks, and then they released her. Her first night home me and Leah spent the whole day with her, trying to make sure she was okay. I could personally tell something wasn't right with her right away, but instead of addressing how I was feeling, I waited until Leah went to sleep in the guest bedroom that night at around midnight. I kissed her on the cheek, then crept into my mother's room.

My mother was sitting on the edge of the bed listening to R. Kelly's *Pray for Me*. She was rocking back and forth with her hands between her legs. She looked like she was hurting something fierce. Her nightgown was pulled up to mid-thigh. I could see scratch marks along her thighs as if she'd been digging her nails into herself and dragging them down her skin until she broke its surface.

I tried to hand her a glass of apple juice. "Huh, drink some of this, Ma. It should make you feel better."

She nudged my hand away. "I don't want that stuff, Jahrome. I need that dope. It's calling me, baby, and I can't hear nothing but it in my head." She rocked back and forth and scratched her neck so hard it bled.

I sat the glass of apple juice on her dresser, then slid beside her. I took her right hand into mine, and kissed the back of it. I was feeling guilty because before I'd gone into my sister room to make sure she was asleep, I'd crept into the bathroom and tooted a gram of heroin myself. The drug had been calling me just as much as it was my mother, but I couldn't let her know that. I had to present a front so she could pick up on my energy and feigned strength. "Mama, I'm here for you. I will not let you fail. Do you hear me?" I asked, wrapping my arm around her shoulder.

She shook her head. "You don't understand what I'm going through right now. I'm itching. My insides hurt. My head is pounding, and my vision continues to go blurry every few minutes. I don't have an appetite. All I want to do is get high. I won't hurt nobody. I just want to be free. I'm starting to miss your father again. It's killing me."

She stood up and dropped to the carpet on her knees. She crawled across it to the spot by her dresser where the dope had fallen after I'd knocked it off of her dresser top a few weeks back. She sniffed along it and rubbed up and down the surface of the carpet with her finger after she sucked it into her mouth. The straps of her nightgown fell off of her shoulders, and I doubted if she even noticed. She was too consumed with her search for crumbs on the carpet.

I sat on the edge of her bed with my head lowered. I didn't know what to say or do. After all, I was feeling like a hypocrite because there I was, high as a kite off of the same drug I was trying to get her not to do. I felt like the worst human being on earth. I was lost with no direction.

She stood up and slowly walked over to me, biting on the nail of her index finger. She looked nervous and a bit worried. "Baby, I need you to help me. I can't take this pain. Can you please get me some work? Seriously. I don't want to go out there and find it myself, but if you don't give it to me, I swear that's just what I'm going to do. I need it so bad." She fell to her knees in front of me and placed her hands on my knees. She looked into my eyes with tears in her own.

I brushed her hands away and stood up. I turned my back to her and lowered my head, feeling sick on the stomach. Snot slowly slid onto my top lip. I sniffed it back up. I could taste the heroin on my tongue and all the way down my throat. It boosted my high just a tad. I felt weak standing there, both emotionally and physically. A man can never know how much he can handle until he sees his mother at her lowest point. My mother was the pillar of our family. Her strength was imperative in order for Leah and myself to know we were strong and had the ability to overcome. Seeing her in such a state of total weakness caused me to start doubting all of my abilities. I stood there, trapped in my inner child, at a lost for words.

She placed her hand on my shoulder and turned me around. "Jahrome, look at me, son. Please. I need you to see me right now and understand where I'm coming from." She fell to her knees again and placed her hands together as if she was getting ready to pray. "Son, I am begging you. I mean sincerely begging you. Rescue me from this nightmare I am trapped in. I can't take this burden. It is too much for me. Either go under your shirt and put one of your bullets right here in my freaking forehead, or give me some work. One or the other! Right now!" she screamed, breaking into tears. "Are you listening to me?"

I looked down into her face with tears sailing down my cheeks. My mother was the only person who could break me down in such a way. To the world, my heart was as cold as ice. But when it came to her, I was as warm as being under a big blanket in the summer time. She was my reason for breathing, my purpose, my heart and soul, and the only one I looked to for strength and determination. But now here she was on her knees, broken, fien'ing for a fix. I knew it was a sight I would never recover from. I wished I could heal her. If God had to take the breath from my body in order to heal my mother, I would have begged him to. I would be her sacrifice.

Leah came to the doorway in just her small pink booty shorts that she slept in and a tank top that was so tight I could see right through it. She rubbed her eyes and stepped into the room. "What is going on in here? Why is she on her knees and crying? What did you do to her, Heinous?"

My mother jumped up and grabbed my sister by the shoulders. "Leah, can you go out and get me some work? Huh, baby? I'm dying right now. I need it so bad," she pleaded.

Leah jerked her head back. "What? Ugh, nall. I thought they were supposed to heal you at that place you were at. It don't seem like it to me." She tried to pry her fingers from her shoulders.

My mother covered her face and started to sob into her hands. She fell to her knees again and bent all the way over until the backs of her hands were on the carpet.

Leah, walked around her body, and slid her arm across my lower back, looking down at her. "What are we going to do, Heinous? She look like she's about to have a nervous breakdown of some sort. Should we call the ambulance?" she asked with her voice breaking up.

I wiped the tears from my eyes and took a deep breath. "Nall, it ain't nothing the ambulance gon' do for her. She's too far gone now. This the only thing that'll work." I went into my pocket and pulled out the quarter ounce of heroin, dropping it on the carpet in front of her. I'd never felt more sick than I did in that moment. I wanted to throw up all over the floor, but I refrained. I took three deep breaths in a row and hugged up on Leah.

She turned around to face me and wrapped her arms around my neck. Now she was crying. "What happened to our mother, Heinous? Where is she? It's like we don't have any parents anymore," she sobbed into my chest.

My mother sat back on her haunches and must've located the dope. She picked up the package and peeled back the layers of the aluminum foil. As soon as she saw the contents, she snapped her neck to look back at me with wide eyes. "Thank you, son. Thank you so, so much." She jumped up and ran to her dresser. She swiped all of the cosmetics onto the carpet and poured a gram on top of it, made two thick lines, and leaned her head to the side, snorting the dope up each nostril. When she finished, she pinched her nose like usual and held her head backward.

I had to get out of the room or I was about to lose my cool. I wound up in the front room, seated on the couch with my head between my legs. I didn't know how to feel about what I'd just done. I felt like I was taking part in the slaughtering of my mother. I was so emotional I knew I needed to kill something, and fast. I didn't like feeling how I was feeling. I didn't want to be that in-tune with my emotions.

Leah came into the living room and sat on my lap. She wrapped her arm around my neck and kissed my cheek, holding her face against mine. "It's not your fault, Jahrome. Please don't beat yourself up over this. She's been through a lot over the past few months. It's her way of escaping it all." She exhaled loudly. "Everybody in Chicago got a parent that's addicted to some drug. It took us a while to become a part of the statistics, but it's finally caught up to us. Ain't nothing we can do about it. It's just this freaking city. You know what I mean?" She lifted my chin and kissed my lips before standing up. "All we have is each other now. It's going to take the both of us to take care of her." She smiled and rubbed my face.

I heard the sound of the window breaking, and then Leah jumped backward into the wall. Her head slammed against it before blood began to pour out of her stomach. Her eyes bugged out of her head. She fell forward onto the carpet, shaking like crazy.

There was rapid gunfire and the sounds of the windows breaking. Big holes formed in the wall of the front room. *Boom. Boom. Boom. Boom. Boom. Boom. Taat-taat-taat. Boom. Boom. Taat-taat. Boom. Boom. Boom. Boom.*

I fell to the carpet and crawled to Leah, turning her over. "Leah! Leah, baby, please don't die. I need you!" I hollered into her face as the front room began to fill up with dust from the drywall as more and more bullets were shot into my mother's crib with no mercy.

Boom. Boom. Boom. Taat-taat. Taat-taat. Taat-taat.

I dropped to my stomach and low-crawled into the guest bedroom, reached into the bottom drawer, and came up with a Mach .90 I'd gotten from Capo. I cocked it and ran back into the front room just as a smoke canister came flying into the room. Quickly, the entire house filled with a thick fog. I couldn't see in front of me.

I heard what sounded like two cars slam on their brakes, then footsteps on my mother's porch. The next thing I knew, there was somebody kicking on her front door so loud it sounded like it was about to cave in. I ran to the window that overlooked the porch and aimed out of it at the five people standing on it with black ski masks over their faces. In the street were two black vans with all of the doors opened on each vehicle.

Bocka Bocka Bocka! Bocka Bocka Bocka! Bocka

Bocka Bocka! I spit with the Mach jumping in my hand. I could hear my mother screaming in the back of the house as the shooting started again from the backyard, and the windows sounded as if they were being shot out.

One of the dudes fell backward as the bullets slammed into his chest. He flew over the banister, and landed on his side, jumped up, and limped to the van with blood leaking out of him.

Boom. Boom. Boom. Boom. Taat-taat! Taat-taat! Taat-taat! The remaining members fired in my direction, sending bullets into the ceiling and the back wall. I dropped to the floor and waited for there to be a short break in their shooting before I countered with more bullets of my own. I popped another dude in the back. He fell into the van, as the rest of the niggas jumped inside of it and stormed away from the curb, firing at my mother's crib on their way off the block.

I ran to the back of the house, choking on the fog. My chest felt like it was on fire. I fanned my hand through the air to try to take away some of the smoke. It was so bad that my eyes were stinging.

"Mama! Mama! Where you at?" I hollered, bent over.

"I'm in here, baby. In my room, under the bed. They back here shooting," she slurred her words.

There was a heavy scent of gasoline. The flames appeared on the side of the house, then all along the back and front of it. "Aw shit. We on fire!" I rushed into her bedroom and looked under the bed, grabbed her wrist, and pulled her up. "Come on, we gotta go!"

Boom. Boom. Boom. Boom. Boom. Boom. More shots fired into the back of the house as the flames soared to a higher level. It got hot real fast. I felt like I was running through an oven. Fire spread all around the carpet.

I had my mother around her waist, rushing to the front of the house so I could get Leah. She was out cold with a small pool of blood around her. I scooped her up into my arms. "Mama, grab ahold of my shirt, and don't let go!" I coughed, inhaling a cloud of smoke that went so far into my lungs it came out of my nose and mouth. My head was spinning. Blood dripped out of my nose.

Boom. Boom. Boom. Boom. Boom. Boom.

I dropped to my knees with my sister in my arms and fell into the flames there. I was burned right away, so I hopped up, stomping my feet. I made my way to the back of the house and to the back door. "Open the door, Mama! Hurry up. The flames are getting bigger."

She coughed and held her arm across her face, turned the locks on the door, and rushed out in front of me, down the stairs. There was the sound of tires spinning on gravel. The back hallway was fully engulfed, the walls on fire and falling inward. My mother screamed and jumped back into me as a huge piece fell in front of us with blue and yellow fire attached to it. It smelled like a burnt Brillo pad. The smoke was thick and black.

"Come on, we gotta go back the other way. We

can't make it through there." It felt like Leah weighed a thousand pounds. My arms were going numb. On top of that, I couldn't breathe to save my life. Every time I took a breath, my lungs were filled with black smoke. I worried that if my sister was struggling to make it, the smoke would choke her to death. I'd heard of children dying in fires from smoke inhalation. I was praying to the heavens my sister and mother didn't succumb to that fate. I didn't really care about me. I just wanted them to survive.

I was also thinking who could possibly be coming at me like this? It seemed as if they were using a strategy straight out of a movie. I knew I had my work cut out for me.

We made it back inside of the house and got halfway through it before the entire living room was engulfed in flamed taller than me. I felt like I was in the bottom portion of the stove that we used to make our toast in. My clothes were drenched and sticking to me and my vest. I was caught in a roadblock. I didn't know what to do.

"The bathroom. Baby, it's our only hope. We can lower ourselves down through the window in there," my mother hollered, then broke into a series of strong coughs that sounded like she was getting ready to cough up a lung. She swung open the bathroom door just as the flames broke out in the kitchen, surrounding the refrigerator. The plastic of the refrigerator fizzed and then popped. There was a bright spark that came from the back of it, and then it fell over with a loud boom.

The window was right above the tub in the bathroom. My mother rushed inside and opened it wide, then she stood on the rim and hoisted herself up and out of it. She dropped to the ground below just as the flames made their way toward me and Leah.

I got Leah out of the window and leaned all the way over, slowly handing her down to my mother. There was blood all over my arms and hands from her wound. As soon as I saw my mother fall to the ground trying to catch her, I wiggled out of the window and fell to the ground beside them.

Chapter 11

Bam!

"Huh, that's a hundred and fifty thousand dollars right there. I need a muthafucking crew of li'l niggas that's ready to murder some shit with no remorse," I hollered, looking across the table at Capo.

"Cool yo' jets, Heinous. I already got that all set up. Brat'll be back in a minute with my li'l Robert Taylor killas. These li'l niggas used to fuck wit' yo pops real tough. Ever since he been gone, they been starving and looking for a come-up. Muthafuckas ready to ride for you, Jo, so don't even trip. It's on." Capo wrapped his arms around the money and pulled it to his side of the table, looking it over.

"Cool my jets? Nigga, my sister been in the hospital for two weeks. They just moved her out of the Intensive Care Unit. My mother scared out of her mind and fucking wit' that dope even worse than before. They blew my muthafucking car up with a grenade. Ain't no room for me to cool my jets, homie." I wiped my mouth and paced back and forth in front of him with a mug on my face. "Nigga, fuck waiting. I'm finna start killing up niggas tonight and every muthafucking night until all of these niggas are dead or sucking my muthafucking dick! I don't bow down to no man. Bitch-niggas gon' pop my sister, shoot and burn up my mother's crib? Really? Aw, nigga, it's on. It's on in every sense of the muthafucking word!"

Capo stood up and nodded, frowning. "Bruh, I

fuck wit' you. Nigga, I'm 'bout whatever you 'bout. If we on some killing shit for the next year, I'ma be beside you every fucking day, ready to bust these guns. All I'm saying is it ain't no use in you riling yourself up because it ain't gon' get us nowhere right now. The best thing we can do is develop a strategy that's gon' exterminate these niggas. An angry man is always the first to die. When your brain is clouded with anger, you can't think logically, only impulsively. You're the smartest nigga in our crew. We need your brains right now. The war is on."

***

Brat came through an hour later and filled up the basement with fifteen young killas from the Robert Taylor Housing Projects. They came in and stood behind her with their hands behind their backs and scowls on their faces. She walked up to me and gave me a hug. "What it do, Jo?"

I hugged her back and shook my head. "I'm fuming. Ready to kill up some shit. These the li'l niggas you picked to stand behind us in these war games?" I asked, looking them up and down. A majority of them had either long dreads or nappy afros. The afros were colored with gold spray, and so were the tips on each of the dreads. Their clothes were rugged, their shoes worn. I could tell they were deep within the struggle, project kids with nothing to live for who knew that tomorrow wasn't promised to them. It was all about the survival of the day they were in. Typical Chicago shit. A nigga'd have to be from the homeland in order to understand it. They didn't have to say nothing from their mouths. I could tell by their demeanors they were killers. They even smelled like death.

I stepped in front of them with an angry mask on my face. "You the li'l niggas my homie chose to fuck wit' me on this murder shit? Huh?" I asked, looking from one to another.

One dark-skinned nigga with gray eyes, and long dreads nodded his head. "We dem Project Assassins. I'm Bam-Bam, and these my potnas. We had a lot of love for your father. He did bidness wit' my big brother before he got killed two year ago. Even after he was gone, your Pops dropped through the 'Jects and made sure my mother had groceries and shit. He did that for a majority of the niggas in my crew. I never got a chance to meet you, but since he yo' old man, we down for whatever for you, homie. Point 'em out and we'll crush them niggas."

"You niggas Crip, Blood, Almighty, Folks, what?" I asked. In Chicago a nigga had to find out where other niggas' loyalties lay right away. I was coming from under the Bloods. If these li'l niggas was Crips or even Folks, I would have been skeptical to fuck with them just because their mobs had been my rivals for so long, even though deep down I really ain't have shit against them groups. I'd always thought gangbanging was stupid, but in Chicago it was the way of life. Either a nigga banged or got his whole family murdered.

Bam-Bam shook his head. "We're family. We rep ourselves. We don't run under no nigga, no star or rag. It's strictly about that paper and loyalty for each other. But now that you putting them chips up and we found out Castro was yo' old man, we'll honor you as our director. Not our chief, just the head our body is currently following behind. It's all love."

He stepped forward and extended his hand. We shook up. His hands felt rough and dry as hell. His knuckles were white and ashy. This was a true Project nigga, one who didn't give a fuck how he looked and would kill a man at the drop of a hat. The kind I needed in my circle.

"A'ight then, it's on. I'ma give each one of you niggas ten gees apiece to fuck wit' me. Along the way we'll accrue more cash, and more will be handed to you. I'm letting you know right now I'm plugging in with you for your murder skills and mentalities. We're set to go at the niggas who killed my old man, and the ones that burned my ol' girl crib down and shot my sister. This shit is personal for me. I need loony niggas that'll cut a baby in half if the mission calls for it. Leave your morals back in the Projects, because ain't no room for them here. I mean that shit. I'm on a bloody, murdering mission. Let's turn the streets red and make muthafuckas feel our pains. You li'l niggas wit' me?" I asked, mugging them.

They smiled in their own different ways and gave me looks that said they couldn't wait to get started.

Chapter 11

"You ready? One, two, three. Go!" I whispered.

Capo took a step back, then kicked the door to Pesos' baby mother's crib as hard as he could. He kicked it so hard he fell on his ass and down two of the stairs of the house. The door caved inward with a loud *whoom* sound. Splinters fell on the porch and all over the welcoming mat.

I came from the side of it and rushed into the house with a black ski mask over my head and my .45 automatic in my right hand. I jumped over the door and into the front room of the house. There, two boys about the age of twelve with video game controllers in their hands looking up at me with eyes wide open. I was about five feet away from them when one of them jumped up and started to run to the back of the house. Brat aimed her gun and fired it twice, putting two big holes in his back. He fell forward and landed on his face. There was a loud scream from the back of the house. Capo rushed past me toward where the screams were coming from.

The other little boy knelt on the ground with his hands over his head in complete submission. I could hear him whimpering and begging us not to kill him. "Please, please, don't kill me. Please," he cried.

Brat nudged past me and kicked him so he fell on his back. "Aye, li'l nigga, shut yo' ass up before I stank you like I just did your friend. You hear me?" she hollered with her foot on his throat.

He continued to cry, folding his lips over his

teeth, as his chest heaved up and down. There was a big wet spot on the front of his jeans. He was shaking as if he was freezing or extremely terrified. The blood from his friend ran over to him and soaked his left side.

When I got to the back of the house, Capo had Pesos' baby mother and two dudes lying on their stomachs with a shotgun at the back of their heads. Bam-Bam and three of his soldiers stood at the ready with their guns pinned on them as well. Bam- Bam moved to the side as I stepped into the back room. He had his foot on Pesos' baby mother's cheek. "Bruh, what you want me to do with this bitch? I'll knock her noodles out her head right now if you want me to."

I snatched her up by her hair and slung her against the wall, pressed the barrel of my pistol under her chin, and forced it upward. "Bitch, where the fuck is yo' baby daddy at?"

She shook her head with snot running over her top lip. "I don't know. He ain't been here in two days. He said he was going out of town, but I haven't heard from him since then, and he ain't answering none of my texts. I don't know why y'all are here but I swear neither myself nor my son have anything to do with it. Please, don't hurt us." She sniffed the snot back into her nose and swallowed. I could feel her shaking. Her knees were going from side to side as if she was seconds away from buckling.

I tightened my grip around her neck until she started to choke. "Bitch, I'ma ask you one more time.

Where the fuck is Pesos? Don't give me that 'you don't know' shit. You're his main bitch and baby mother. You know something. Spit that shit out," I ordered with my face only a few inches from hers.

Tears ran down her cheeks. She started to whimper, and then she spit in my face as if the devil had entered into her. "Fuck you. I ain't telling you shit, bitch-nigga. Do what the fuck you gon' do. I'm riding for my nigga until the death."

She swung and tried to knock the gun out of my hand, kneeing me in the right side of my thigh, just missing my nuts. I struggled to hold her up against the wall. *Boom.* Her head jerked on her neck, as the bullet from my gun crashed into her face and blew the back of her head off.

I dropped her to the floor, and wiped her plasma out of the holes in my mask. As soon as she dropped, she defecated on herself. Its strong scent entered the room.

Capo cocked his shotgun. "Then fuck this li'l nigga, too. It's a family affair, my nigga." *Boom.* He blew the head off of one of the men they had lying face down, leaving a big hole in the back of his skull. The scent of gunpowder and burned brain matter wafted into the atmosphere so heavy I could taste it.

The other man tried to get up and run out of the room. He didn't make it past the doorway before Bam-Bam blocked his path and put four big holes in his chest. He stood over him and applied three more bullets to his face. Blood from all three of the victims ran out of their bodies and soaked the carpet so bad it ran into the hallway and along the sides of the wall.

"Let's get the fuck out of here. That bitch-nigga ain't here right now, but we gon' find his ass. Until we do, it's murder-murder all around the Windy. That's on my mother," I stated, stepping into the hallway to find Brat.

She sat on the little boy's back with her gun pressed into his jaw. "What y'all do? Y'all kilt everybody back there?" she asked, looking up at me in anticipation.

I nodded. "Hell yeah, you already know what it is. Muthafucka clapped at my mother's crib and tried to burn her shit down. From here on out, it's no mercy." I stood over her and the little boy.

She nodded her head. "Shid, say no mo'. It's over for his li'l ass." She pressed the barrel harder into his jaw, finger sliding alongside the trigger.

"Wait, shorty!" I rushed over and grabbed her arm, pulling her up and off of him.

"What's good, nigga? Let me lace his li'l ass," she snapped, trying to get a clear shot at him. I was standing in her way.

I shook my head. "Nall, this that nigga son, I assume. Is that right, li'l nigga? Pesos yo' pops?"

He was curled into a ball, crying his heart out. He looked up at me with snot all over his lips and tears dripping off his chin on down his neck. He nodded his head. "Yeah. That's my dad. What did he do to y'all for y'all to do this to our family? It's not right," he cried, dry heaving and choking on his spit.

I snickered and knelt down. I didn't feel shit from

all of the crying he was doing. As far as I was concerned, had I not been there to save my mother and sister, both of them would have been dead. Even in that moment my sister was lying in the hospital, wounded my bullets I was sure came from Pesos' guns, or from one of his shooters. Fuck his son. I was aiming to make his bitch-ass feel the same heat my sister was feeling.

"Say, li'l nigga, you tell yo' punk-ass daddy that Heinous said the war is on, and it ain't over until one of us is in the dirt. Tell that bitch-nigga he brought this shit to my family first, so it's an eye for an eye. You got that?" I asked, looking down on his crybaby-ass.

He nodded his head. "Yes, sir. I do. Can I go to my mother now?"

I cackled and smacked him across the face with my gun. He fell on his back. I pressed the gun to his right shoulder and pulled the trigger. *Boom.* Then I did the same with his left and both kneecaps, leaving him a bloody mess. He hollered from his hobbled position, in obvious pain and agony.

"Tell yo' father what the fuck I said!"

Brat came and placed her hand on my shoulder. "Let's get the fuck out of here, bruh. I hear sirens. Them people on they way."

***

Yani massaged my back with Cashmere Gold massage oil. She kissed along my spine and applied pressure to my lower back. "I been missing you like crazy, Daddy. I've been worried about you in these streets." She finished her massage and lay beside me with her face on my shoulder. I could smell the peppermint of her breath.

I still had the murders from earlier that day on my mind. The way Pesos' baby mother spit in my face before I blew the back of her head off, the little boy left in the middle of the floor with a bullet in each of his extremities. I was thinking I should have killed him instead of leaving him alive to get the word back to his old man. The entire murder scene was all over the news already. They was making it seem as if the family had been attacked by terrorists. I was wondering how long it was going to be before Pesos clapped back or the police got on my ass? I had to find a way to prepare for both, and I was having regrets on how I handled shit.

"Baby, you know you ain't gotta worry about me out there. Worrying ain't gon' do nothing but make you sick. When it's my time to go, your worrying ain't gon' stop me from going, so why waste your time on that emotion?" I placed my big hand on her thong-clad ass. The pink string separated her globes. Her thick thighs were spread just enough for me to see the lips pressed against her crotch band.

"That shit is easier said than done, Heinous. I'm crazy about you. I mean, I understand you gotta do what you have to, but that doesn't mean I can't be worried about my man. Life without you would suck. All these niggas out here are so damn foo-gazy. Not

cum all over my mouth." I slid my middle finger into her asshole, worming it in and out.

"Ooh, Daddy. Daddy, what you do to me. It feel so good, Daddy. It feel so fucking good." She ran her tongue all over her lips and pinched her clit, pulling on it with her thumb and forefinger.

I licked all over her fingers before moving them out of the way and going to town on her pussy, sucking both lips, then sticking my tongue as far into her as it would go. I slapped her on the ass and licked up and down her middle. "Give Daddy that salty shit. Cum in my mouth, baby. Cum. It's good. I wanna taste you."

"Uh! Daddy! You gon' make me! You gon' make me! Aw, shit! I'm 'bout to cum! I'm 'bout to cum all over yo' mouth, Daddy!" She screamed and opened her thighs as far as they could go while I feasted on her from the back like a monster. Her pussy squirted and hit my lips. I grabbed both sides of her ass cheeks and opened them while my lips sucked on her pearl, tongue pulling it outside of her brown lips.

She shook like crazy and tried to kick me away from her. "Daddy! Daddy, it's sensitive. It's sensitive!" she cried, clawing at the bed sheets.

I forced her to the mattress and licked around her anus, sliding my tongue in and out of her backdoor, sucking on her opening.

"Give me some of my baby. I want some of my baby right the fuck now." I pulled my dick out of my boxers and kicked them off. I stroked my pipe up and down, running the head along her lips. "You want some of Daddy, baby? Huh? Tell Daddy you need this dick just as bad as I need this pussy right now."

She placed her face down, and tilted her ass up. "Fuck me, Daddy. Kill this pussy. You know how you gotta do me." She pulled her bra under her titties, exposing them, and pulled on the nipples, playing with them.

I slid my head into her hot opening and pulled it back out. Her juices coated me. The scent of her pussy was already heavy in the air. I could taste her on my tongue and all down my throat.

Her hole stretched around my invasion. Her back arched as I entered her deeper and deeper. She tensed and shook just a bit, digging her nails into the back of her thighs. "Uh. Uh. Daddy, stop playing wit' me and go as deep as you can. I. Uh, shit!"

I grabbed her hips and slammed into her pussy, working it in and out of her as I rubbed all over her full moons. The cheeks jiggled with every forward thrust. When I pulled backward, her lips sucked at me, her juices dripped off my balls and onto the sheets below us. I got to attacking that good pussy, loving the feel of it. I felt like I was diving into the depths of her soul. Her insides was like a raging inferno, its lava thick and intoxicating. Her skin crashed into mine and created a clapping sound that added to my bliss. I held her right titty in my hand and worked her like I would be fucking for the last time. And due to the war I was dead smack in the middle of, for all I knew it could have been my last time, so I wanted to make the best of it.

"It's good, mama. It's good. This pussy good, baby. Aw, fuck, it's so good." I groaned, plunging into her faster and faster. The bed rocked back and forth. I smacked that ass and squeezed the hefty cheeks. She was so thick I couldn't help it.

"Daddy, cum in me." She bounced back into me. "Cum in me, Daddy. Shit! I wanna. Feel. It." She lowered her head and crashed into me over and over. Her thighs vibrated. She grabbed a handful of the sheets and pulled them off the bed before biting on them. She screamed in the back of her throat.

I grabbed her hair and yanked her head backward. "Nall, bitch. I wanna hear that shit. Scream for Daddy. Scream for me!" I growled, speeding up and fucking her so hard I was hurting my abs. That big ass spread across my stomach, and every time she bounced back I could feel her asshole on my belly button, scorching it. I didn't know how much longer I could last. I smacked her as hard as I could on her ass and slid two fingers into her back door.

"Fuck, Daddy. That's how you fuck me! That's how you fuck yo' baby girl. Aw, shit, I'm cumming again. I'm cumming! Kill it!"

I got to hitting that shit like a jackrabbit, fucking her as fast as I could, smacking them cheeks as I went. My dick slid in and out of her womb. I felt my head going sensitive, and then I was cumming along with her with my eyes shut as tight as I could get them. I felt like my climax came from all over my body. I got to shooting off in her and whimpering at the same time before falling on top of her ass, out of breath.

***

Yani lay on top of my body with her thick thigh draped across my waist. Her eyes were wide open, staring up at me. She smiled and shook her head. "Daddy, I love you so much. I wish we could just leave Chicago and never look back. The world is so much bigger than this ratchet-ass city. We can't do nothing but continue to lose here. Can't you see and understand that?" she exhaled loudly and ran her hand along my abs.

"Yeah, Boo, I hear you. We are gon' bounce from this bitch, but first I gotta handle my bidness. I can't let what happened to Leah, my pops, and my mother just ride. Muthafuckas gotta reap what they sow. It's just the way it is. I'm my family's first and only line of defense."

She nodded. "I know, Daddy, but what if something serious happens to you? Then who will defend them?" She rose on her elbow to look into my eyes.

"I don't think about that type of shit. I ain't dying no time soon. When I do, I'ma make sure my family is in a safer place and got everything they need. I can't leave them out on a limb. I'm more of a man than that." I didn't even want to think about me getting fucked over and murked in the streets. It's not that I was fearful of death. I worried how vulnerable the women in my family would be without my presence. I couldn't stand for some nigga to target them just to really shit on my grave after I was gone. I knew I had to get my family out of Chicago. It was their only hope of survival.

"Daddy, I would go crazy if something happened to you. I mean, I'm a woman and I can stand on my own two feet, but it's just that you're all I know. It's been that way since high school."

I pulled her all the way on top of me and made her lay her head in the crux of my neck. There was something about holding a small woman that did it for me. Ever since we were shorties, I'd always loved how she felt within my arms. Yani was more special than any other woman I'd ever been with because I trusted her, and we had been through so much. When I thought about the aspect of having a wife, I saw her as my One. I knew for a fact I could wake up next to her every single morning for the rest of my life and be happy. She was my completion, and it also helped she went both ways. I'm just being honest.

I kissed her on the forehead. "Baby, you gotta stop speaking that shit into existence. Now, I'ma be good. I know how to handle myself in that jungle of life. I know I gotta get y'all up out of this city, so that's my priority, along with murdering this nigga Pesos and company. Just let me handle my bidness, and in the meantime you start getting your shit together so we can shake this city. I gotta have you alongside me when I make that transition. Every thug needs a down-ass bitch, and ain't no other female out there more down than you." I pressed my lips against her forehead and held them there. I loved this woman more than I knew I did. She was my portion.

"Well, Daddy, as long as you know. That's all that matters to me. I'll do whatever you want me to do, but just know I see bigger than the ghetto. I wanna be somebody in this world, so whenever we leave, you gotta stand beside me and help me to achieve my goals so I can be an asset to you as well as myself. The streets aren't going to provide for us forever." She kissed my nipples and smiled. "I can't wait until we leave. How long do you think it'll be? I'm ready to go right now, you know, once I close a few business deals that can be transferred to wherever we're moving to. Speaking of which, where are you trying to go? Have you even decided yet?" She reached between my legs and squeezed my dick that was lying up against her cat.

"I wanna go out east. I'm sick of the Midwest altogether. I ain't been feeling this part of the states for a long-ass time."

"Where, though, baby? The east coast is huge. And what would we do out there?" she asked, looking into my eyes with interest.

I shrugged my shoulders. "I don't even know yet. I gotta master this current predicament I'm in, and we'll go from there. You know the way my mind works. I gotta complete one task at a time."

"Well, Daddy, long as when we get to wherever we're going, you stand behind me and motivate me to be the best woman I can be. I'm riding with you.

You'll always be able to count on me."

Chapter 12

"Sit up, Leah. You gotta eat something or you're going to continue to be sick. Now, take a bite of this sandwich." I held the grilled chicken sandwich up to her lips.

She sat back on the pillow of her hospital bed and shook her head. "I don't want it. My stomach still feels funny, Jahrome. Can't you understand that?" she said through a hoarse voice.

"Please, baby, just take a little bite for me. You can't be on a feeding tube forever, it's not healthy. Now, I need you to just try." I brushed her hair out of her face and placed the sandwich to her lips again. I lay my cheek against hers. "Come on, ma."

She sighed. "Damn, you just gon' force me, huh?" She opened her mouth and took a small bite, chewing with her eyes closed. She had a sour look on her face that told me she was struggling to consume the small portion she'd just taken into her mouth. I was proud of her for the effort.

I continued to stroke her long, pretty hair, feeling sick deep within the pits of my stomach because my sister was laid up in a hospital bed, struck by a bullet that may have been meant for me. Our whole lives I'd always done everything I could to protect her. To see her injured, and me not having been able to prevent it, made me feel like the worst person in the whole world. I was wishing I could have inhaled that bullet in her place. It just wasn't fair.

The more I looked down at her, the worse I felt.

I kissed her cheek. "I love you, sis. I swear to God, I do."

She pointed at the small table on the side of her hospital bed. "I love you, too, Jahrome. Hand me that juice box. My throat drier than a desert right now." She tried to clear it loudly and held her throat, swallowing her spit before groaning.

I poked the straw into the juice box and held it to her lips. "Here you go, sis. Take your time, okay?"

She sucked the juice through the straw a little at a time. Between swallows she'd take her mouth away from the straw and take a deep breath, then she'd place the straw back to her lips and repeat the same process.

Seeing her in action was breaking my heart down the middle. I should have been there to protect her. It was all my fault. I hated myself. She was my little sister. My heart. The first of two females I'd been taught to love. Our whole lives it had always been me and her. There was nothing I couldn't go to my sister about. I'd broken down in front of her on numerous occasions, and she'd done the same with me.

"Jahrome, I wanna get the fuck out of Chicago. I feel like if we don't, another one of us is going to die. To be honest, I'm afraid it's going to be you." She looking up at the ceiling, then slowly trailed her eyes over to me.

I got frustrated. "Damn, why everybody keep saying that shit?" I sat her juice box on the table and turned my back on her. I was trying to calm myself down by taking deep breaths. I didn't want to snap at my sister. especially since she was already in a vulnerable state. I knew she didn't mean any harm by what she'd just said, but it was like Yani had already beat that dog into the ground. I didn't want to hear a whole other spiel about somebody taking my life and why I shouldn't have been out in the streets or still in Chicago.

I wasn't the type of man to run away from my problems or enemies. I felt if a muthafucka wanted to take it there wit' me, then I would meet they ass head-on and with every bit of firepower I could muster. There was no ho in my blood. To pack my shit and flee Chicago would have made me feel like a pussy for the rest of my life. I was born in the Windy City and raised by the guttersnipes who roamed it. I didn't fear no man, nor death. If I was gon' die, I was gon' die with my head held high and my gun smoking.

"Jahrome, calm down, because I'm not about to get on you. I can tell you're already irritated, and I don't want to add to what you're already feeling, but I can't help stating the obvious. I'm scared, big bruh. I've been scared for a very long time, but I've kept it to myself." She held out her arms for me. "Come here. I need you."

I waved her off. "Not right now, man! This shit driving me crazy. I can't let this nigga get away with what he did to you. This punk put a bullet in your belly and burnt Mom's crib down, and that's after he hit me up and kilt our father. What kind of man would I be if I didn't stand on my two feet and fight for this family when I'm all we've got on the front lines? Help me to understand this shit, Leah!"

She shook her head as tears ran down her cheeks. "Please stop hollering at me, Jahrome. I'm so weak right now, and I need you. Now get your ass over here and hold me! Shit! I fucking need you, nigga, damn!" She frowned and clutched her stomach, waited to see what I was going to do.

I made my way over to her. I hated to see my sister cry. I sat on the bed and wrapped my right arm around her small frame, kissed her temple, and then her cheek. "I'm sorry, Leah. I know I'm fucking up, but I don't know what to do. I can't let this nigga fuck over our family. Now you done got hit, Moms ain't got no crib to call her own, and she doing that heroin like ninety going north. Our family has been torn apart because of one nigga. Am I supposed to just let that shit ride? Tell me, sis."

She laid her head on my shoulder and closed her eyes. "I can't do this if you're dead, Jahrome. I can't lay my fucking head on your shoulder if you are no longer here!" She broke into a fit of tears. "I don't care about what he's done to us. We can't change the past. All we can do is master our future, but we won't have a future if we keep on doing the same shit that got us screwed over in the past. How much more killing is it going to take? I was this close to losing my life." She held her thumb and forefinger together in the sign of an inch. "Had that bullet been three more centimeters to the right, I would have been laying on a slab in the freezer in the morgue."

As she was talking, I imagined what that would have looked like and almost passed out. As strong as I was, I knew I wasn't capable of withstanding the death of my sister. I needed her. I loved her way too much, especially since heroin seemed as if it was taking over my mother's life. I didn't know if she would ever be the same again, and that crushed my soul.

"You don't have to prove anything to anybody, including yourself." She grabbed my face and looked into my eyes. "Nigga, I know you'll fuck over this punk. I, of all people, know what you're capable of, but listen to me. We need to get out of this city and get as far away from Illinois as possible. We need a fresh start. The Reaper seems to be sitting in the cut, waiting on our bloodline to be picked off. We've been given second chances, all of us, with the exception of Daddy. We need to utilize these second chances and get the hell out of here before it's too late. I love you, and I need you alive. Screw those streets. See me, and not them."

"What about me?" my mother spoke from the couch. She raised her arms far above her head and yawned, took the blanket off of herself, and made her way over to us. "Y'all act like I'm dead already. Y'all ain't said nothing positive about me this whole conversation. Damn, am I even still alive?" She sat on the other side of Leah.

Leah kissed my cheek and hugged me to her possessively. "Mom, I'm not saying it like that. I just know how his mind works. He needs to focus in on something he can cling to. Jahrome loves me to death. One of the reasons he's looking to go so hard is because of what happened to me. I love him for that, and it makes me feel so special, but if I can get him to redirect that powerful negative energy he has from what has taken place into a positive space, we'll be able to prosper and my brother won't lose his life in these streets. I'm not strong enough to endure losing him, Mom. I'm just not." She held me tighter, her cheek against my own.

My mother scratched her arm until blood appeared in the cracks. "Y'all don't love me no more, I can see it. Leah, you're already expecting for it to just be you and him. I can tell by the look in your eyes. I could have died, too, the other night. You're not the only victim here, Leah." She looked at her arm and dabbed at the blood with her pointer finger.

I held out my other arm. "Come here, Mama, 'cause it ain't like that. I love you with all of my heart, just like I love her. Y'all both are my first loves. It's my duty to protect and cherish you two. A man is stronger when there are strong women around him who care about him. I am an animal because of you two."

My mother walked around the small hospital room and came under my left arm. She kissed my cheek and laid her head on my shoulder. "Thank you for saying that, baby. I needed to hear that because I've been feeling so down on myself. I've lost my way, and I need to find the road back to me. But right now I'm lost. I lost everything in the fire. I don't know what to do other than these damn drugs." She exhaled and clung to me tighter. "But I do understand where you're coming from, Leah, and I agree with you. We need to get out of this city. It's not safe here, and there is no benefit for us being here. I feel it within my gut that if we don't leave, something worse is going to happen." She scratched at her arm again.

Leah snuggled her face into my neck and closed her eyes. "You need to pray on this, Jahrome. Pray, talk to God, and see where He leads you. He will never leave, nor forsake you. If there is one thing our mother taught us, it was that."

"Yeah, you see? I know I'm falling off because I should have been the one giving you that advice, not your sister. Sometimes it's refreshing to see you kids actually listened to me. I have to find my way back. I can't go out like this."

I held both of them with a billion thoughts going through my head at one time, all of them screaming loudly, but no thought louder or more clear than the one telling me I needed to get my family out of Chicago.

Hood Rich

Chapter 13

School Boy placed the suitcase full of money on the table and opened it. He sat back in his chair with a big smile on his face. "Nigga, you got the city on edge after what y'all did to Pesos' kids. Every muthafucka in the city looking for you and your crew. Pesos gave me this paper up front for your head. Half is his, and the other half is from Lloyd. I guess you stanked his li'l niece and that fool Tommy Kid. Them niggas fronting like they ain't on edge, but I swear to you they spooked, my nigga. The question is, what you gon' do about it?" he asked me.

He separated his heroin and got ready to toot a gram up his nose. I grabbed the red straw and tooted a thick line from my own pile of work. It had been three weeks since we'd murdered Pesos' baby mother and shot up his kid. The city was on fire. I was getting all kinds of reports that he'd placed a million-dollar bounty on my head. Everybody and their mother was trying to cash in on it. I was guessing since School Boy was known for tracking niggas down and killing them in bloody fashions, Pesos and Lloyd had come together so they could bring me to my bloody end. That fucked me up in the head. I couldn't do nothing but get high. The world was spinning too fast for me at the moment. I felt sick and dizzy.

I cleared two lines and sat back in my chair, pinching my nostrils. I could feel the dope shoot up to my brain. Residue dripped down my throat. My heart was pounding so hard I felt like it was going to bust. "You took the money, so that must mean you're my slayer." I curled my lip at him and rested my hand on the handle of my pistol.

I was ready to buck this bitch-nigga down. I wanted to see what his brains looked like leaking out of his face. I'd never liked him to begin with. I needed to know what he was up to. He had my anxiety going through the roof. Every time I was around him, I was always waitin' for the unexpected to happen. I didn't trust him as far as I could throw him. I knew he was a shyster. I knew he had to have something up his sleeve. He was one of those cocky, way-too-sure-of-himself-type of niggas. I knew if I could get him to running his mouth, he would expose his hand. If I could get him to do that, then I could find a way to capitalize off of his own strategy.

"Yeah, nigga, they dropped them money bags for me to slay you, so I guess you can call me that. But that ain't the way shit gon' go. Just between me and you though, nigga, if I wanted you dead, you'd already be that way. You see, I know what type of nigga you are. I know you're a relentless killer just like me. I know the longer you are alive, your opposition doesn't stand a chance. If you were my enemy, I wouldn't lay my head on a pillow until you were out of the game."

He sucked his teeth, grabbed the bottle of Tanqueray, and turned it up. He took five big swallows, burped, and set the bottle down on the table so hard some of the liquor popped up and spilled over the top. He wiped his mouth and looked across the table at me with a scowl on his face.

We were in the attic of his crib with a red light bulb screwed in. The attic was stuffy. I was sweating down my back, my hand on the handle of my pistol, ready to blow this nigga's face to the moon.

"Nigga, if we were enemies, you would never get that far. I don't give a fuck what you doing out here in these streets. When it comes to me, shit ain't sweet. Why the fuck you take the bag of money if you ain't on shit wit' me?" I asked, separating the heroin on my plate into two thin lines.

He sat back in his seat and looked me over for a long time. He ran his tongue across his teeth. "This shit is all so simple. You got these so-called tough niggas with their backs against the wall. To the point, they're willing to pay however much money just to have you knocked off. But instead of going to just anybody-type niggas, they brought this bread to me because they know how I get down. When niggas in the game come to me for assistance, that means shit is real. That li'l stunt you pulled wit' Pesos' family got the game on its heels. Nigga ain't think nobody had the heart to go at that chump the way you did. Now that you have, they're spooked, and they want yo' ass taken out by the best. That's me. But fuck that. What we're going to do is use this shit against them to really milk their stashes.

I finished tooting my lines and felt the heroin course through my system. I was high in a matter of seconds. I'm talking fucked up and ready to kill something. The red light in the room was making me think about murder and death. That fuck-nigga School Boy looked like a victim to me. But I had to keep him talking. The worst thing a man could ever do in the game was run his mouth to a nigga like me.

I sat back in my chair and mugged him. "Fuck, you think you calling shots over me or something, nigga? Huh? I'll have you know I don't take orders from no nigga. I'm my own king. You sitting here making it seem like I'm your fucking video game or something." I clutched the handle to my pistol even tighter. I felt I was seconds away from blowing his shit back.

He smiled and tooted four lines of heroin before sitting up and grabbing the bottle of liquor. "Look, nigga, I don't need to call shots over you, but we had a deal, and it's in your best interest to see this deal through, especially right now." He snickered to himself.

"Oh yeah, right now especially, huh? Tell me what's so important about right now?" I asked scooting my chair back just enough to be able to raise my gun from under the table.

"Because right now you got the whole of Chicago looking to do something to yo' ass. I'm the only muthafucka that's making sure you stay ahead of the game and keeping breath in your lungs. If not me, then who? Think about it."

I scooted my chair all the way back. It scratched against the floor loudly as I hopped up and cocked my pistol. "Fuck-nigga, if not you, then me. You ain't keeping me alive, homeboy. I'm alive because I'm a muthafucking soldier. Get that shit through yo' head. The only person that can kill me is God. not none of these bitch-ass niggas that's putting money on my head. You sitting here like you all high and mighty and shit. You ain't got no power over me, Jo. Check that shit in right now."

School Boy looked up at me and lowered his eyes. "Nigga, you either about to pull that trigger and send me on my way, or you gon' sit yo' ass down so we can have a polite conversation where we can both benefit from this chaos ensuing around us. Now, I ain't got shit against you. I actually need you. I'm man enough to say that. But I can't have you pulling bangers out on me and shit. I ain't one of them other boys, Jo. You should already know that." He pulled on his nose and sniffed loudly.

The heroin in my system was telling me to buck his ass down, to fill him with lead so I could see how his blood looked pouring out of him. Whenever I was doped up, I yearned to murder and to watch somebody being murdered. I was in love with the gore of it all. If the heroin didn't bring out my murder fascination, it made me horny and want to fuck like crazy.

I looked down on School Boy from my position. "Nigga, tell me what you're up to," I demanded. I was about to sit back down because I was on the fence about killing him. Almost every part of me told me to smoke his ass or it would come back to haunt me. There was only me and him in the house, so I could have smoked him and went on my way. Nobody would've been the wiser, and shit would have been over with.

But a huge part of me just had to know where he was going with things.

"A'ight, nigga, listen." He scooted his chair to the table and interlocked his fingers on top of it while he looked up at me with snot dripping out of his right nostril. He sniffed it back in and swallowed it. "Them niggas are so spooked over how you handled Pesos' family – you know, leaving his son to tell the tale – that Lloyd and Pesos came together and gave me five hundred thousand dollars up front for your head. The deal is for a million in all. Anyway, I wanna flip the script on their ass. I got the drop on Lloyd. I want you to fuck him over. Cut that nigga's head off and leave it beside his body. I'm serious. That's how I want the authorities to find this bitch-nigga so it can go viral. Once you knock him off, all of his niggas that are already flirting about coming under my umbrella will convert to me and my new version of the Bloods. On top of that, I got his treasurer on my payroll. We kill Lloyd, and then empty all of his safes. I'll hit your hand and see to it you have everything you need on Pesos to take his ass out of the game. I know once he finds out how Lloyd was spilled, he's going to up the ante. He'll put up at least three million dollars. All this cash will go directly to you. On top of that cash, you'll be able to murder this nigga in any fashion you want to get revenge for what he did to you and your people. In the meantime, I'll snatch up his niggas and bring them under me. Your last order of business will be to slay Lost Boy. Right now I'm his right-hand man. If he goes down, then I'm in command of his troops. We'll make it seem like I'm on the hunt for you and you've got wind of it, because you're going to kill my baby mother anyway. That was our original deal. Ain't nobody gon' be thinking we're working together, and in the meantime I'll be sowing up the city, cornering each and every market, because that's what it's all about for me. You feel me?"

I scrunched my face, and placed my right hand on the table. "And, nigga, how is all of this benefitting me more than it is you?" I asked, looking into this evil nigga's black-ass face.

"I never said it would benefit you more than me, but you will be able to get your revenge, and it's four million dollars in cash in it for you. In fact," he stood up and pushed the suitcase full of money across the table toward me. "Huh, before you came I added an extra five hundred thousand dollars to that pot. It's one million total, and it's all yours. See it as something like a signing bonus. I ain't your enemy, Heinous. I'm fucking wit' you the long way. Until the end, my nigga. I need Lloyd dead by tomorrow night. I'll send you the information on the hit. I already know what bitch he gon' be laid up with. One of my queens." He rubbed his chin and laughed to himself.

I dragged the case across the table and fished through it. It was filled with hundred dollar bills, all small faces. That money had to be from back in the day. Probably had been tucked in the back of a wall somewhere. Nevertheless, it was a million dollars, and in order to get my women out of the city and to safety, I had to have this cash. Even if I would have had to blow that nigga's head off for it.

I nodded my head. "A'ight, cool. Send me everything I need for Lloyd. I'ma handle that shit tomorrow night, the right way.

***

Leah crawled across the bed and laid her head on my chest after kissing me on the cheek. She winced in pain as she situated herself against me. "Damn, this shit still hurts, Jahrome. But I'm getting better. I can feel it." She picked up my big arm and placed it around her small body.

I allowed her to snuggle up into me before I held her close. I kissed her on the cheek. "You're a warrior, li'l momma. Pretty soon you won't feel a thing. It took me a few weeks to get over my injuries. Just keep fighting and leaning on me for support. I got you."

Yani slid into the bed and kissed the back of Leah's neck. She trailed kisses along her spine, brushed her hair out of the way, and kissed her cheek in the same spot I had. "Hey, what about me? I'm here for her, too, Heinous." She poked out her bottom lip at me.

I smiled. "Aw, shorty, I ain't mean to leave you out, but she know what it is. This my li'l baby, right here. I'm her shield from here on out." I kissed Leah's forehead and rubbed her back. "Ain't that right, baby sis?"

She looked up at me and smiled. "You already know it. I love you, Jahrome. You've always been there for me." She looked over her shoulder at Yani. "You been holding me down too, though, big sis. I love you to death. You know what it is."

Yani pursed her lips. "Uh-huh. I guess I'll take that, even though it seems a li'l watered down. Since Heinous healing you in his own way, let me do my thing. I think it's about time you got a little release." She rubbed along her back and pulled her nightgown above her waist, exposing the black thong underwear underneath. She rubbed all over Leah's booty cheeks. "Daddy, lean back and let her lay on you while I get her right real quick. Shid, I'm trying to be in her heart, too."

I pulled Leah on top of me and wrapped my arms around her lower back. Her lips were against my cheek. I could feel her heart pounding in her chest. "It's okay baby, just chill and let Yani do her thing. It's a family affair in this muthafucka."

Leah nodded her head and moved her hips from side to side to better position herself for Yani. Her face slid into the crux of my neck, her hot breath along my collarbone. I looked over her shoulder at what Yani was getting ready to do.

Yani pulled her gown all the way up and left it around her lower back. She pulled Leah's panties to the side, and her pussy popped out from between her thighs. Yani got down on her stomach and sniffed Leah's pussy. She moaned deep within her throat. "Damn, it's something about y'all genes and the scent it gives off that drives me crazy." She opened her lips, revealing her pink, then slid her tongue into the crack and licked all the way up and then down it, slurping it so loud the sounds were starting to do something to me. I was already high as a kite. My dick was hardening. I tried to move Leah off of me, but she dug her nails into my sides.

"Sis, you gotta get up. My shit getting hard as hell," I said in a raspy voice.

"So what? I feel it. And what? Just stay here with me. I still need you right now." She rested her lips against my neck. "Uh! Yani, that feels good. Please don't stop."

Yani took two fingers and slid them into Leah's pussy while she sucked on her clitoris. Her fingers ran in and out of her at full speed. I could hear the slouching of her juices as Yani manipulated her. She made sucking noises and smacked her lips.

"I ain't gon' stop until you cum. This pussy taste so good. I can't get enough of it." She attacked it with a vengeance, holding the lips wide open.

Leah humped backward into her fingers, moaning loudly. Her wet lips grazed against my neck. Her tongue swiped at my skin before retreating back into her mouth. "It feel so good, Jahrome. It feel so fucking good. She got me so wet," she groaned. She leaned all the way forward and spread her thighs further apart.

168

I was feeling guilty as hell and a bit bogus, because while she was humping back and forth, her body weight on my piece was stroking it up and down. I wanted to push her off of me so bad, but once again the dope had me feeling some type of way. On top of that, the sounds coming from Yani's lips and her pussy were driving me insane. I know I should have been turned off by the fact she was my sister, but in all honesty, I just wasn't. Me and her had been flipping bitches together since we were little kids. We'd gotten close, but had never fucked around with each other, though I'd be lying if I said I hadn't thought about it. Not to the point I would actually do something about my curiosity, but it had crossed my mind before. I'm just being honest.

Yani continued to eat her like a champion. She reached between our bodies and pulled my dick out of my boxers. Leah actually lifted up so she could remove it through the boxers' hole. Once he was free, he throbbed in the air before Leah laid back on him and continued to hump back and forth on Yani's tongue.

Leah bit into my neck and moaned out loud. "Aw, fuck, Yani. I'm about to cum, sis. I'm about to cum." She lay against me and rubbed her face against mine before she got to shaking like crazy.

Yani dug her face deep into her crack and got to eating her pussy up. She rubbed all over Leah's big booty, opening the cheeks and fingering her asshole. "Cum! Cum! Cum, Leah. It's alright."

Leah screamed and dug her nails into my back.

169

"Shit. Shit. Shit. It feel so good." She scooted upward and ground her pussy against my dick, moaning louder and louder. I could feel her wetness allover my pipe. It was so much that in a matter of seconds my entire lap was drenched in her fluids.

"Put it in me, Jahrome. Please. Who gives a fuck? Just put it in me. I need it," Leah groaned, digging her nails into my chest and dragging them down my abs.

I humped upward and moved her off of me. "Nall, ma, we ain't gon' get down like that. You just feeling vulnerable right now."

Yani slid between my legs and took ahold of my dick, stroking it up and down. "Shit, I thought y'all been did something like that, anyway. Ain't nobody here but me. I ain't gon' say shit." She sucked my dick into her mouth, running her lips up and down my long, thick pole like a porn star. I was loving the feeling.

Leah crawled over to me and laid one of her hands on my stomach. The other one was between her legs. "I'm so fucking horny, Jahrome. I think it's them pain pills that got me fien'ing for some pipe. Let's just do it, man. Who gives a fuck?" She placed her cheek against Yani's, stuck her tongue out, and licked the head of my dick.

Yani sat back and stroked it up and down for her. "G'on 'head and put it in your mouth, Leah. Break that barrier. It won't be no turning back then." She pinched Leah's hard nipple through her gown, making her moan.

Leah took my dick in her hand and stroked it two times before sucking it into her mouth. She groaned around it and took her lips all the way to my nut sack. Then she popped it out and looked down on it with eyes wide open.

I pushed her hand away and stood up with my dick jumping up and down. There were all kinds of veins going through it, and the head was a bright purple, fully engorged and throbbing. "I ain't finna let her do that shit. We'll both regret that in the morning."

Even though I said that, I was riled all the way up. I knew if I'd let Leah finish doing what she was doing, we were going to fuck, and there would be no coming back from that. I didn't know how that would make me feel, or her either, for that matter. I didn't want to risk my relationship with my sister. She meant the world to me. I mean, I can't lie and say it wasn't tempting, because it was. Leah was not only strapped, but she was fine as hell. It took that moment for me to finally admit that truth. Had I fucked her, I was sure we would have been in trouble.

"Bae, I ain't never seen yo' dick that long before. Look at it. It's way past your navel and almost to your lower chest. You want her pussy just as bad as she wanna give it to you." She kissed Leah's lips as Leah stuck her hand down the front of Yani's panties.

My dick got to throbbing even worse. I was losing my willpower. Leah pulled Yani's panties all the way down her thighs before sticking her face between them. Her ass was in the air with her thighs spread, her pussy on full display. The sex lips were reddish-brown and fully engorged. A trail of juice leaked out of them and slid down her left thick thigh. Yani slid her hand between her thighs and opened her lips for my view.

I shook my head and squeezed precum out of my dick's head.

There was a knocking on the front door that snapped me out of my zone. I threw my dick back inside of my boxers, and grabbed both of my .45s, cocking them.

Chapter 14

Upon opening the door, I saw Brat sitting outside. Brat leaned back in her cherry-red 2019 Mustang sitting on 28-inch, 188-spoke, diamond-cut bullets. They were old school, but her whip was fresh off the lot. My father had given her the rims for her birthday, and today was my first time seeing them.

"The bounty is up to two million dollars, Heinous. Most of the niggas we grew up with trying to cash that bounty in. I don't know who to trust." Brat frowned and pulled on her nose. "I been tooting cocaine all night. Scared to close my eyes."

I sat with my head back against the headrest of the Mustang. "I been fucking with That Boy, that heroin. The same shit that's taking my mother away from me. I'm addicted now. My body gotta have it." I lowered my head and shook it. "I almost fucked Leah, too. I think this dope got me tripping."

It was eight o'clock at night, and the sun was just going down. A car slowly rolled past hers going the opposite direction. Brat placed her finger on the trigger of her Mach .11, ready to air some shit out. Both of my guns were already on my lap. We were both on point, living on edge. Chicago life, I guess you could call it.

The car rolled past and turned from the block. Brat turned to me and shrugged her shoulders. "I thought y'all been fucking anyway. Didn't you tell me that y'all used to flip hos together?" she asked, lowering her body in her seat.

I nodded. "Yeah, but we ain't never did shit. The most we've ever done was probably kiss, but that's as far as it's ever gone." I looked at her like she'd lost her mind. "Dang, so you telling me this whole time you thought her and I was doing the do?"

"Shit, yeah. I thought when you said y'all flipped hos together it meant y'all was having threesomes together. But whatever, nigga. The bounty is two million. What are going to do about it?" she asked, looking over her shoulder and then back out the front of her windshield.

"We gon' fuck over this nigga Lloyd first. Half of that two million put up is by him. We gotta alleviate his bitch-ass, and then knock off that fool Pesos. Once both of those heads are severed, we'll be in the clear. The last order of bidness will be School Boy. I don't trust that chump."

Brat lowered her eyes and slumped lower in her seat as another car slowly drove down the street in our direction. The car passed us and parked a few houses down on the opposite side of the street from Yani's crib. Brat picked up her Mach and lowered her window.

I had both guns up and cocked. I rolled down the window on my side, and sat on the windowsill, looking across the street to see who was about to get out of the car. If they even looked like a threat, I was emptying both clips. I rested my elbows on the roof of Brat's car, ready to fire.

The interior lights came on in the car. I saw there was a female getting out of it. She opened her door, stepped out, and then took her baby out of the car seat in the back. Because all of the streetlights on Yani's block had been shot out, she was not able to see us lurking. Had she been a threat, she would have been filled with holes. I watched her as she carried her baby up the stairs to her house and inside.

I slid back into my seat. "Like I said, we gon' fuck over this nigga Lloyd tomorrow night and take it from there. Once he's out the way, our next mission is Pesos."

She nodded. "Lost Boy gotta go, too, though. I been getting word from some of the Bloods that he still feeling some type of way about how we got down on him a few weeks back. Ain't no telling when he gon' strike, so I say we hit his ass first. You know how the game go. I been eating his baby mama pussy, and she been feeling like getting even with his ass ever since he left her for her cousin. That dumb nigga married the bitch and everything, and didn't give a fuck that she sold pussy. And now she ain't fucking wit' him because she caught him fucking School Boy baby mother in their bed. It's crazy, but you know that hell hath no fury like a woman scorned. Both bitches want that nigga out the picture. They got tabs on all of his paper that's put up. Greed is a muthafucka."

I smiled. "Ain't it always? Well, keep working your end, and we'll see what comes up with that nigga. In the meantime, we gon' fuck over this Lloyd nigga and go from there. You understand me?"

She nodded. "Nigga, I'm probably the only one

that do. I got you, fool. It's all love. I'll be ready tomorrow."

***

School Boy called me up the next night at two in the morning. I was lying in the middle of Yani and Leah. That night I'd watched them fuck each other into oblivion while I watched from afar. As soon as they were done, I got behind Yani and hit that pussy for a whole hour with my eyes closed, remembering all I'd seen them do. Leah watched us and held Yani's pussy lips open for me while I rammed her like crazy. I swear I had never cum so many times and so hard in my entire life.

I hadn't been asleep for more than thirty minutes when School Boy's call came through.

Three hours later, Bam-Bam and Brat were tying Lloyd's hands up and pulling them over his head so his bonds could fit atop the hook that hung from the ceiling of Brat's basement. The redbone School Boy had used to set him up was also bound and gagged. She lay on her side on the concrete floor with her knees to her chest. She moaned into her gag and shook her head from right to left.

I shook up with Brat and stepped past her with a steak knife in my hand. I stopped in front of the hanging Lloyd and looked his fat ass over. He was about 6'2" tall and an even 300 pounds with a long perm that was too outdated. He was ass-naked and smelled like booty and musk. His chest was full of curly gray hairs.

I ripped the tape off of his mouth. He let out a gasp of air and smacked his dry lips together. "You bitch-ass nigga! Who gave me up?" he snapped.

That caught me off guard. I was expecting this fuck-nigga to fold or beg for his life, but to my amazement he did none of the above. I had to honor his moxie.

I swung a right hook, crashing it into his jaw, and sliced him across the chest wit' the steak knife, digging deep as I trailed it across the length of his shoulders. He flopped around on the hook, blood skeeting out of his wound.

"Ah, you muthafucka! I'ma kill you for this. Who gave me up?"

"Why you want me dead, nigga?" I asked, stepping back in front of him. I needed some answers. I knew what School Boy was saying, but I wanted to hear it from the horse's mouth before I stanked his black ass.

"You kilt my son. You and yo' punk-ass posse killed my baby. My only son. That's why I wanted yo' head, nigga. Then you laced my niece and right-hand man. What the fuck was I supposed to do?" he asked with blood running down his stomach. His bottom lip was split in two. It looked like it had been clipped with scissors.

I smiled. "So, it is true. Okay, that's all I wanted to know. Hell yeah, I smoked yo' punk-ass son. Fuck that li'l nigga. Ah-ha!" I cackled in his face. "Then I sent yo' fat-ass niece on her way, along with Tommy

Kid. It is what it is. I should've waited, that way all of you muthafuckas could've had your funerals together. But it's good." I took a step back, then lunged forward, implanting the knife deep into his shoulder and ripping it downward. It sliced him wide open. I felt his skin pop as the knife entered into him.

He struggled against his bonds, so Bam-Bam, and Brat ran over and held him still. "Argh! This nigga! Muthafucka!" he hollered. Spit shot out of his mouth and landed on his chin, mixed with blood.

I was high and angry. I kept on imagining my sister lying in the hospital with a bullet in her belly. I knew he had to have had something to do with it. I pulled the knife out of his chest and slammed it back into him over and over again. "Who shot my sister, bitch-nigga? Who. Shot. My. Muthafucking. Sister? Who. Did. It? Who? Who? Who? Who?" I growled, stabbing him again and again with no mercy. The blade went in and out of his body, creating big holes in his torso. There was so much blood leaking out of him that it pooled around my Jordans.

There was no way he was going to answer my question because, by the fiftieth stab, his head was laying against the top of his chest. His eyes were wide open.

"Get his punk-ass down and lay him on the ground," I ordered. I traveled across the basement and picked up the chainsaw, pulling on the cord to rev the engine. It started with a *vrrrr*!

Brat and Barn-Barn laid him flat out on his back with a puffy coat under his neck to stop me from slicing into the concrete beneath him. I knelt on one knee and brought the blade of the chainsaw down to the skin of his neck, pulling the trigger to make the blade spin faster and faster. As soon as the chain touched his skin, it broke it and sunk into his flesh. I held it while it vibrated in my hand. His blood popped up and splattered the walls as I took my time severing his head from his body.

Before it was all said and done, Brat had put one in the head of the female School Boy had used to set Lloyd up. We drove their bodies to Golden Gate Park on South Eberhart and 130th Street. Then I hit School Boy's phone.

***

My mother sat on the bed in the hotel room, nodding in and out. She ran her fingers through her hair and licked her dry lips. "I'm tired, baby. Mama so tired. I feel the weariness all in my soul." She took the syringe and stuck it in the thick vein in her forearm. As she pushed down on the feeder, her eyes closed and bottom lip quivered.

I sat on the loveseat across from the bed with watery eyes. I didn't know when she'd made the transition from tooting to shooting, but somewhere along the way she had, and it was breaking my heart. I didn't know what to do or say. I was lost.

Leah came over and sat on the arm of the loveseat. She wrapped her arm around my neck and let her hand rest on my chest. "She losing a lot of weight, Jahrome. Look at her. She must've easily lost twenty pounds."

"I ain't been eating. Don't think I've eaten a full meal in at least two months. Don't none of my clothes fit no more. I don't ever have an appetite. I don't even know why the good Lord woke me up this morning." She lay back on her elbows with her eyes closed. A slight smirk came across her pretty face.

Leah shook her head. "What should we do? Should we force her to go back to rehab? Maybe put her in one that'll actually help her this time, or what?" She sank down on the couch until she was sitting on my lap with her cheek against mine.

"Mama, you think you ready to go to rehab for real this time?" I asked, looking over at her. I was on the verge of breaking down. Not only was the scene with my mother getting to me, but after Lloyd's murder, the streets were really calling for my head. There were rival gangs clicking up in search of me. They wanted to find and annihilate me. I hadn't known Lloyd had been the plug on heroin for eighty percent of the dealers in the city. Now that he was gone, Chicago was headed for an ugly drought that would cost millions of dollars in lost dope boy wages. Kingpins were coming together in an effort to find and finish me in any way possible.

"I ain't thinking about no damn rehab. Them white folks can't do nothing for me that the good Lord can't do. This here heroin is all I got, especially since y'all abandoned me." She lay all the way on her back and covered her face with her hand.

I patted Leah on the side of the butt and made her stand up. She looked back at me as if something was wrong. "What's the matter?" she asked.

I shook my head and went over, kneeling beside my mother's feet. "Mama, why do you feel like we've abandoned you? Don't you know I would never leave your side? You're my first love."

She sat up with tears pouring down her face. "I shouldn't be, son. I ain't got that much longer. God told me that in my dream last night. He said he's calling me home soon, and I better be ready. So, until He does, I'm gon' do this here dope and let my hair down. I ain't eating no more. What's the use?" She exhaled and squeezed her eyelids together.

I stood up and pulled her to her feet, wrapped my arms around her, and held her close to my heart. She smelled like must and a hint of unwashed kitty. There was the scent of deodorant along with sweat. I imagined that instead of washing her body, she'd just applied deodorant and kept it moving. I mean, I didn't know for sure, but I knew that most heroin addicts didn't like washing their bodies because they felt that every time their pores were opened, it allowed the dope to seep out of their system. I thought it was a crazy theory, but to each their own.

"I love you, Mama. You're my life. You and Leah. Don't you ever tell me to not care about you or to write you off as if you're already dead. I ain't going to. If something was to happen to you or my sister again, I would have a nervous breakdown and lose my mind. Everything I do, I do it for the both of you. I mean that."

I held her and looked over my shoulder at Leah. Leah smiled, kissed her hand, and blew a kiss at me. She used to have a habit of doing that when we were little kids. Somewhere along the lines of growth and development she'd grown out of it, or so I thought.

"I'm just giving you a heads-up, baby. I don't want you and your sister to have to face anymore blindsides. That can kill a person. I'm tired, honey. Your mother is so tired and so broken that I don't know what to do."

I lifted her in the air and held my forearm under the back of her thighs. "Leah, go run her bath water. I'ma bring her in there in a second."

Leah jumped off of the couch to follow my directives. She held her arm around her stomach and winced in pain, paused for a second, took a deep breath, then headed into the bathroom.

I bounced my mother up and down as if she was just a child. Then, in the best singing voice I could muster, I began to sing a Boyz II Men song to her with my lips against her cheek.

You taught me everything.
And everything you've given me,
I'll always keep it inside.
You're the driving force in my life, yeah.

I whispered the entire song in her ear while I held her. As a kid I'd always sing the song to her whenever she felt down, and it never failed to make her happy. My mother was a very emotional woman when you got to the bottom of her soul. She was proud and headstrong, but underneath it all she was a very emotional queen, and I loved her with every fiber of my being. She was my truth.

She cried and cried while her right arm remained around my neck, the must from her armpit growing stronger and stronger. But it didn't bother me. She was my life source. Even in her worst state, all I saw was beauty. She was a goddess, and I knew I could get her to see her worth again. I just needed to remove her from Chicago so we could get a fresh start.

"It's ready, Jahrome. Do you want me to do anything else?" Leah asked, holding her stomach. She looked like she was about to pass out. She held onto the wall for balance.

I frowned. "What's the matter with you, sis?" I asked, carrying my mother over to her.

She shook her head and smiled. "Oh, nothing. I was feeling just a bit dizzy. I'll be okay. Let me go and sit on the bed while you get her clean. Don't worry about me." She staggered from the wall to the bed, sitting on it with her jaw puffed out.

"A'ight, ma, call me if you need me. Lay down for a minute and I'll be out later. I love you."

"I love you, too, Jahrome. And that sounds good." She got all the way into the bed and laid her head on the pillow.

Hood Rich

Chapter 15

My mother undressed and stepped into the tub. She sat down and allowed the water to consume her. "I knew one day it would be you taking care of me, Jahrome. Even though you were one of those little boys that loved to fight. You were always crazy about your mother. Most of the fights you got into at school was because somebody had said something about me. You didn't play them damn 'Yo' Mama' jokes. No suh, my baby been crazy about me." She smiled and shook her head.

I lathered the towel, and washed under her arms, and then across her chest and her back. I loved my mother so much. To see her in such a state was killing me. As I washed her arms, I could see the dirt coming off of her skin. It was depressing for me.

"I'm still crazy about you. That's why I gotta get you and Leah out of the city and onto greener pastures. I got a million in cash to make it happen. When we get to our new spot, I'ma cop you a church so you can do yo' thing. We gotta bring that dream of your back into the forefront. I think it was your strength. Everybody should have a dream to hold on to. It gives a person a reason to strive forward. Stand up."

She stood up and allowed me to scrub her body from front to back and head to toe. I let the filthy water out and ran fresh water into the tub.

She sat down in it and sighed. "What is your dream, baby? You've never told me what it was."

"My dream is to move you and Leah out of Chicago. For us to get to a safer place. And then I wanna open a few businesses, and maybe a Boys and Girls club. There wasn't any role models around for me when I was coming up. Had there been any positive ones, I wouldn't be the animal I am. So, I guess I want to save a few kids, you know. Give them a chance before they don't have one." I lathered her long, pretty hair and turned on the shower. "Run your fingers through yo' scalp, Ma. It's a lot of dandruff in there." I took a step back and watched her do her.

After she finished, she stood up and I dried her off, picked her up, and got ready to carry her back into the hotel bedroom, but stopped in the doorway when I saw Leah lying face-down on the floor, unmoving.

"Aw, shit!" I lowered my mother and nearly broke my neck to run into the other room. I knelt down and pulled Leah into my arms, tapping her on the face. "Baby? Baby? Baby? Wake up. Wake up." I laid her on her back and started to do CPR. "Mama! Mama! Call the ambulance. Call 911. My sister ain't moving. She ain't moving, Ma!" I checked her heart to see if the CPR had helped. Her faint breathing gave me a bit of hope, yet terrified me at the same time. I jumped up and grabbed my car keys, then rushed back to her side.

My mother came out of the bathroom holding her chest. "Baby. My heart. My heart, baby." She fell to her knees, holding her chest. Sweat poured down the side of her face. She bit into her bottom lip before

186

falling on her back and having a seizure.

"Ah, fuck! Lord, not right now!" I rushed to my mother's side and held her up. She shook in my arms with spit fizzing around her mouth. Her eyes rolled into the back of her head. Her legs kicked wildly. The vein in her forehead was more prominent than I had ever remembered it being.

"Mama! Mama! Mama! What's the matter? What's wrong with you?" I tapped her on the cheek, and opened her mouth wide to see if she was trying to swallow her tongue.

Her tongue was lying up against the side of her mouth, so that wasn't a problem. She got to shaking so bad she slipped out of my hands and fell to the carpet, coughing up white foam. I started to panic. I had my sister across the room on the floor, unmoving, and my mother in front of me, choking and flopping all over the carpet.

I jumped up, ran into the bathroom, and grabbed my mother's carryall bag from the side of the tub. I saw there was a syringe and a small quantity of heroin on top of the toilet. I guessed that before my mother had come out of the bathroom, she'd taken the time to shoot some more of the poison, and now she was paying for it.

I knelt down and unzipped her bag, rifled through it until I found the small box of Narcan and retrieved it. I knew my mother had always been a very smart and cautious woman, even through her drug addiction. There was no way she would have been unprepared for something as severe as this.

187

I took the nasal spray out of the Narcan box. The medication would reverse whatever the heroin was doing to her body.

I nearly tripped over my own feet getting back into the room where I'd left her. Once there, I held her shaking body up and carefully positioned her face so I could spray the contents into her nose. She continued to shake for a few more minutes before she calmed and only her right leg continued to kick.

I rushed across the carpet and knelt by my sister's side, placed my ear against her lips, and heard nothing. My heart dropped into my stomach. I felt sick. I felt like the world was coming to an end. I couldn't breathe. I was lost. On the verge of becoming hysterical.

I fell onto my back with tears rushing out of my eyes. I couldn't believe it to be truth. My sister could not be dead. She was my everything. I couldn't fathom the loss.

Snot ran out of my nose, and I started to perform CPR on her all over again. "Come on, sis. Come on, sis. Breathe. Breathe. Please don't die on me. Don't you die on me. I need you. You are my life," I cried, pumping on her chest.

I pinched her nose and breathed into her mouth. Her chest rose and fell. I laid my ear back over her mouth. Nothing.

Now I was starting to freak out worse than before. I repeated the entire process, looking over my shoulder at my mother. She lay still on her back, unmoving. Sweat poured down the side of my face, and we were in a well air-conditioned room. I was losing my mind, I felt.

I blew as hard as I could into Leah's mouth. Her chest rose in the air and then fell. She jerked and then started to cough with her face frowning. Those were the happiest noises I'd ever heard in my life.

I leaned down and hugged her in my arms. "I thought you were gone, Leah. I thought I had lost you. I love you so fucking much!"

"My stomach hurts, Jahrome. You gotta get me to a hospital. I can't take the pain." Her eyes rolled into the back of her head, then she fainted.

I placed my ear by her mouth and felt that she was breathing ruggedly. I kissed her on the forehead and laid her back on the floor. A circle of blood formed on her blouse, right in the section of her abdomen where she was shot.

I ran across the room and laid my ear on my mother's mouth. Her breathing was raspy and labored, but nonetheless she was breathing, and it was enough to give me hope.

I threw my bulletproof vest on, followed by a shirt, put both .45s on my waist, then picked up Leah and carried her down to my Ford Explorer. I sat her in the back seat and placing the seatbelt around her.

I rushed back up the stairs of the hotel and carried my mother down next. Slobber ran out of her mouth and along my arm. She jerked again and again in my arms, and that worried me. Before I closed the door, I stopped and made sure she was still breathing.

I slammed the door to the Explorer and got in the

driver's seat when Brat's Escalade pulled into the parking lot of the hotel. Instead of her parking in between the yellow lines, she parked crooked, then jumped out with a worried expression on her face. The first thing I saw was that her white T-shirt was bloody, along with the jeans she wore.

She jogged away from her truck and headed toward the front door of the hotel. I blew my horn and rolled down my window. "Brat! Brat! Shorty, I'm over here. What's good?" I yelled, starting the ignition.

She stopped and looked at me, shaking her head before jogging to my truck with tears in her eyes. "They just kilt my mother, Heinous. My mother, my brother, and both of my nieces. I don't know what to do! I don't know what the fuck to do!" She screamed and dropped to her knees in the parking lot.

"Fuck!" I slammed my hand against the steering wheel. "Damn, Shorty, that's fucked up. You already know I'm riding wit' you. I gotta get them to the hospital first. My mother back there OD'ed. I think my sister suffering from that gunshot wound to the gut. I gotta get them both to the emergency room, like, ASAP." I looked down at her with sweat dripping off of my forehead.

Brat lowered her head between her legs. Tears ran down her cheeks. Her eyes were puffy, and she smelled like death. "Did you just hear what I said, Heinous? I lost my mother, brother, and my nieces. I'm finna kill them niggas, man. I finna tear this muthafucking city up. What make it so bad is I saw that nigga Lost Boy's Rolls Royce rolling off the block right before I pulled up on my mother's street. I know he had something to do with it. It's killing me, man."

She lay flat on her stomach and broke into a fit of tears. I'd never seen her that way. I could only imagine what she was going through.

I didn't know what to do as the sun shone bright in the afternoon sky. On one hand I wanted to get out and console her because she was my right-hand man. I knew she needed my arms wrapped around her. I was a male, and had all of that shit happened to me, I would have needed her to hug me up a little, too.

But then there was my people, too. They still had a chance of surviving. I couldn't waste any more time. I had to get them to Cook County Medical Center or there was a huge possibility I was going to lose either one or both of them, and I couldn't let that happen.

"Brat, get up and follow me to the hospital. Come on. Let me get them inside, and then you and I can get on bidness," I promised, feeling like my back was against the wall. I was seconds away from pulling off on her, no matter what she did. I didn't want to do that, but she was kind of forcing my hand.

Brat slowly got to her feet. She looked up at me with red eyes. Her shoulders were slumped inward, her white t-shirt matted to her frame by blood. Sweat was all over her face, along with blood.

"First Castro, now my whole family, Heinous. What the fuck are we gonna do?" She turned her back and made her way to her truck with her head lowered.

Before she could make it there, two all-red Chevy Caprice Classics turned into the lot with niggas sitting on the windowsills. Automatics were in their hands. They had red rags draped across the bottoms of their faces. Their cars slammed on their brakes.

"Brat! Get the fuck out of the way," I yelled, throwing my truck in park and hopping out with both .45s in my hands, spitting at the hittas. *Bocka! Bocka! Bocka! Bocka! Bocka!* The guns jumped in my hands. The shells spit out of them and rolled along the pavement of the parking lot.

Brat turned toward them and lifted up her shirt, grabbing a .40 Glock and busting. *Boom. Boom. Boom. Boom. Boom. Boom.*

Taat-taat! Taat-taat!

They spit at both of us. Their bullets rocked the side of my truck and busted out the back passenger window. My mother's head fell against the door. Her eyes were closed tightly.

I was ducked down, but hopped up during their pauses of shooting. *Bocka! Bocka! Bocka! Bocka!* I shattered their windshield.

One of the cars stepped on its gas and stopped right in front of my truck before the shooters started to let off round after round. I jumped back into my truck and ducked down. The windows exploded. The truck vibrated and rocked from side to side.

I threw it in reverse and stepped on the gas, storming backward and slamming into a parked car. *Whoom*! The sound of metal crunching resonated loudly in my ears.

More shots slammed into my truck. My windshield shattered into my lap. I threw the truck into drive and stepped on the gas, slamming directly into the side of the Chevy Caprice. *Bam*! My truck took the Chevy about three feet. The hittas jumped out of the whip with AKs in their hands just as the other one pulled behind me, trapping me in. I could see they also had assault rifles in their hands, ready to finish me.

I was caught, stuck in a sticky situation.

To Be Continued...
Kingpin Killaz 2
Coming Soon

Submission Guideline

Submit the first three chapters of your completed manuscript to ldpsubmissions@gmail.com, subject line: Your book's title. The manuscript must be in a .doc file and sent as an attachment. Document should be in Times New Roman, double spaced and in size 12 font. Also, provide your synopsis and full contact information. If sending multiple submissions, they must each be in a separate email.

Have a story but no way to send it electronically? You can still submit to LDP/Ca$h Presents. Send in the first three chapters, written or typed, of your completed manuscript to:

LDP: Submissions Dept
Po Box 870494
Mesquite, Tx 75187

DO NOT send original manuscript. Must be a duplicate.

Provide your synopsis and a cover letter containing your full contact information.

Thanks for considering LDP and Ca$h Presents.

Kingpin Killaz

BOW DOWN TO MY GANGSTA

By **Ca$h**

TORN BETWEEN TWO

By **Coffee**

BLOOD STAINS OF A SHOTTA **III**

By **Jamaica**

STEADY MOBBIN II

By **Marcellus Allen**

BLOOD OF A BOSS **V**

By **Askari**

LOYAL TO THE GAME **IV**

By **T.J. & Jelissa**

A DOPEBOY'S PRAYER **II**

By **Eddie "Wolf" Lee**

IF LOVING YOU IS WRONG... **III**

LOVE ME EVEN WHEN IT HURTS

By **Jelissa**

TRUE SAVAGE **V**

By **Chris Green**

BLAST FOR ME **III**

By **Ghost**

ADDICTIED TO THE DRAMA **III**

By **Jamila Mathis**

LIPSTICK KILLAH **III**

CRIME OF PASSION **II**

Hood Rich

By **Mimi**
WHAT BAD BITCHES DO **III**
KILL ZONE
By **Aryanna**
THE COST OF LOYALTY **II**
By **Kweli**
SHE FELL IN LOVE WITH A REAL ONE **II**
By **Tamara Butler**
LOVE SHOULDN'T HURT **III**
RENEGADE BOYS **II**
By **Meesha**
CORRUPTED BY A GANGSTA **III**
By **Destiny Skai**
A GANGSTER'S CODE III
By **J-Blunt**
KING OF NEW YORK III
By **T.J. Edwards**
CUM FOR ME **IV**
By **Ca$h & Company**
GORILLAS IN THE BAY
De'Kari
THE STREETS ARE CALLING
Duquie Wilson

Available Now
RESTRAINING ORDER **I & II**

Kingpin Killaz

By **CA$H & Coffee**

LOVE KNOWS NO BOUNDARIES **I II & III**

By **Coffee**

RAISED AS A GOON I, II, III & IV

BRED BY THE SLUMS I, II, III

BLAST FOR ME I & II

ROTTEN TO THE CORE I III

By **Ghost**

LAY IT DOWN **I & II**

LAST OF A DYING BREED

BLOOD STAINS OF A SHOTTA I & II

By **Jamaica**

LOYAL TO THE GAME

LOYAL TO THE GAME II

LOYAL TO THE GAME III

By **TJ & Jelissa**

BLOODY COMMAS I & II

SKI MASK CARTEL I II & III

KING OF NEW YORK I II

By **T.J. Edwards**

IF LOVING HIM IS WRONG…I & II

By **Jelissa**

WHEN THE STREETS CLAP BACK I & II III

By **Jibril Williams**

A DISTINGUISHED THUG STOLE MY HEART I II & III

LOVE SHOULDN'T HURT I II

RENEGADE BOYS

Hood Rich

By **Meesha**

A GANGSTER'S CODE I & II

By **J-Blunt**

PUSH IT TO THE LIMIT

By **Bre' Hayes**

BLOOD OF A BOSS **I, II, III & IV**

By **Askari**

THE STREETS BLEED MURDER **I, II & III**

THE HEART OF A GANGSTA I II& III

By **Jerry Jackson**

CUM FOR ME

CUM FOR ME 2

CUM FOR ME 3

An **LDP Erotica Collaboration**

BRIDE OF A HUSTLA **I II & II**

THE FETTI GIRLS **I, II& III**

CORRUPTED BY A GANGSTA I & II

By **Destiny Skai**

WHEN A GOOD GIRL GOES BAD

By **Adrienne**

A GANGSTER'S REVENGE **I II III & IV**

THE BOSS MAN'S DAUGHTERS

THE BOSS MAN'S DAUGHTERS II

THE BOSSMAN'S DAUGHTERS III

THE BOSSMAN'S DAUGHTERS IV

THE BOSS MAN'S DAUGHTERS **V**

A SAVAGE LOVE **I & II**

Kingpin Killaz

BAE BELONGS TO ME

A HUSTLER'S DECEIT I, II

WHAT BAD BITCHES DO I, II

By **Aryanna**

A KINGPIN'S AMBITON

A KINGPIN'S AMBITION **II**

I MURDER FOR THE DOUGH

By **Ambitious**

TRUE SAVAGE

TRUE SAVAGE II

TRUE SAVAGE **III**

TRUE SAVAGE **IV**

By **Chris Green**

A DOPEBOY'S PRAYER

By **Eddie "Wolf" Lee**

THE KING CARTEL **I, II & III**

By **Frank Gresham**

THESE NIGGAS AIN'T LOYAL **I, II & III**

By **Nikki Tee**

GANGSTA SHYT **I II &III**

By **CATO**

THE ULTIMATE BETRAYAL

By **Phoenix**

BOSS'N UP **I , II & III**

By **Royal Nicole**

I LOVE YOU TO DEATH

By **Destiny J**

Hood Rich

I RIDE FOR MY HITTA

I STILL RIDE FOR MY HITTA

By **Misty Holt**

LOVE & CHASIN' PAPER

By **Qay Crockett**

TO DIE IN VAIN

By **ASAD**

BROOKLYN HUSTLAZ

By **Boogsy Morina**

BROOKLYN ON LOCK I & II

By **Sonovia**

GANGSTA CITY

By **Teddy Duke**

A DRUG KING AND HIS DIAMOND I & II III

A DOPEMAN'S RICHES

By Nicole Goosby

TRAPHOUSE KING **I II & III**

By **Hood Rich**

LIPSTICK KILLAH **I, II**

CRIME OF PASSION

By **Mimi**

STEADY MOBBN'

By **Marcellus Allen**

WHO SHOT YA **I, II**

Renta

Kingpin Killaz

BOOKS BY LDP'S CEO, CA$H

TRUST IN NO MAN

TRUST IN NO MAN 2

TRUST IN NO MAN 3

BONDED BY BLOOD

SHORTY GOT A THUG

THUGS CRY

THUGS CRY 2

THUGS CRY 3

TRUST NO BITCH

TRUST NO BITCH 2

TRUST NO BITCH 3

TIL MY CASKET DROPS

RESTRAINING ORDER

RESTRAINING ORDER 2

IN LOVE WITH A CONVICT

Coming Soon

BONDED BY BLOOD 2

BOW DOWN TO MY GANGSTA

Hood Rich

www.ingramcontent.com/pod-product-compliance
Lightning Source LLC
Chambersburg PA
CBHW070703280626
47159CB00022B/1794